FROM SHADOW LAND
AND OTHER GHOST STORIES

FROM SHADOW LAND
AND OTHER GHOST STORIES

JULIA S. HARRIS   JENNY WREN   SILVERLEAF

Corella Press is an initiative of the School of Communication and Arts at The University of Queensland. 'Corella Press' and the Corella Press logo are unregistered trademarks of The University of Queensland.

From Shadow Land and Other Ghost Stories
Copyright © University of Queensland's Corella Press, 2021

From Shadow Land; Or A Traveller Returned by Julia S. Harris
Published in by South Australian Chronicle (Adelaide, SA: 1889–1895) on 17 December 1892
A Man and His Money by 'Jenny Wren' (Nellie Cruttenden)
Serialised in The Daily News (Perth, WA: 1882–1950) on 30 September, 2 October, 3 October, 4 October, 5 October, 6 October, 7 October, 9 October, 10 October, 11 October, 12 October, 13 October, 14 October, 16 October 1899
M'Kenzie's Ghost by 'Silverleaf' (Jessie Georgina Lloyd)
Published by The Sydney Mail and New South Wales Advertiser (NSW: 1871–1912) on 14 April 1883

Published by Corella Press
School of Communication and the Arts, The University of Queensland
Email: corellapress@uq.edu.au
URL: https://www.austlit.edu.au/austlit/page/14512405

All rights reserved. Without limiting the rights under copyright reserved above, no part of this publication may be reproduced, stored in or introduced into a database and retrieval system or transmitted in any form or any means (electronic, mechanical, photocopying, recording or otherwise) without the prior written permission of both the owner of copyright and the above publishers.

Cover illustration and logo by Kathleen Jennings | www.KathleenJennings.com
Cover Design by Peter M. Ball | www.PeterMBall.com

Printed by IngramSpark
ISBN 978-1-922560-00-1 (Print)
ISBN 978-1-922560-01-8 (Ebook)

CONTENTS

NOTE FROM THE EDITORS

The editors seek to honour the authors of this anthology and their work by bridging the gap between twentieth-century readers and nineteenth-century storytellers. To this end, inconsistent punctuation has been regulated, spelling discrepancies have been amended to meet contemporary Australian standards, archaic and obscure terms have been explained in the end glossary, and language with the potential to offend has been moderated.

The stories inside this book reflect the development of the Australian ghost story and make powerful social critiques. Harris's tragic "From Shadow Land; Or a Traveller Returned" takes place in England but may be interpreted as an Australian woman's critique of the gendered violence and xenophobia masked behind the stately English manor. "A Man and His Money" is a more hopeful perspective on this theme, where kindness and female friendship overcome the colonial greed and classism represented by haunted estates. Finally, in Silverleaf's work we see the distinctive Australian landscape emerge as integral to the story. Although humorous, the frightening encounters with the natural world in "M'Kenzie's Ghost" may represent early colonial anxieties associated with the harsh reality of an Australian landscape that had promised prosperity. We hope that you enjoy following the development of a uniquely Australian voice as our stories shift from tragedy to romance to humour, and from the grand but haunted British manor to the uncanny Australian bush.

The first printings of these short stories can be accessed at Trove, the online archive of the National Library of Australia, at www.trove.nla.gov.au.

INTRODUCTION

KATHLEEN JENNINGS

The ghostly tales inside *From Shadow Land and Other Ghost Stories* will ensnare you with their horror, their romance, and occasionally, their light-heartedness. From brooding manors to isolated tracks, these stories will transport you to landscapes of love and tragedy, prejudice and obsession… and paranormal encounters.

This compelling collection, the fourth in Corella Press's historical mystery and crime series, preserves the voices of three women who, like their subjects, haunt Australian literary history. While the name of Silverleaf (Jessie Georgina Lloyd) is still heard, 'Jenny Wren' and Julia S. Harris have largely been forgotten. But over a century later, their fiction remains alluring and relevant to contemporary readers.

From Shadow Land and Other Ghost Stories, containing three gripping and entertaining mysteries, is the final instalment in Corella's electrifying collection of recovered nineteenth-century Australian mystery fiction. It is the product of many hours of tireless research, transcription, and editorial work by Corella Press interns, all students at the University of Queensland, who have unearthed and revitalised the serialised work of nineteenth-century women writers. True to Corella's mission, this collection preserves

Cruttenden, Harris, and Lloyd's authorial voices while reintroducing them to a contemporary audience.

Harris, Cruttenden, and Lloyd made themselves heard in Australian publishing in a period when women's writing was often severely undervalued, and their words should not be lost to history. While their published stories are clearly relevant to the development of a vibrant Gothic genre in Australia, these works also contribute to other significant strands of Australian literary history: from the evolution of outback tall(ish) tales, to the threads that would be picked up by contemporary romance writers.

"From Shadow Land; Or A Traveller Returned" (Harris, 1892), "A Man and His Money" (Cruttenden, 1899), and "M'Kenzie's Ghost" (Lloyd, 1883), are contrasting and complimentary variations on the ghost story. Each provides insight into the authors' social reality (and ideals), their explorations of upper-, middle- and working-class experiences, and—read together—their illustration of the developing Australian identity against a backdrop of colonisation. But they are also written to *entertain*. These are tales (within tales) of passion, tragedy, affection, fear, rational investigation, irrational obsession, overbearing parents, scrub cattle, garrulous drovers, fiscal irresponsibility and the rewards of kindness. And several ghosts.

I have always been enchanted by the potential of the Australian Gothic—the struggle of writers to express both the beauty and the uncanniness of landscapes, the toying with fairy tales as a template for conveying a strangeness out of place, the immense space into which secrets can be dropped, and the silences that should be filled with voices. Part of my love for the genre stems from the way the mode and mechanisms of the Gothic can be used both to confront and avoid the concerns that haunt contemporary Australia—and the consequences of both choices. And, less earnestly, the childish thrill of a good ghost story. I've tangled with these fascinations in my own short stories and debut novel, as well as in my art, and having illustrated Corella Press' covers for the last three years, I'm incredibly proud to have contributed to this collection. I believe *From Shadow Land and Other Ghost Stories* is the perfect triptych to end Corella's mystery and crime series.

So read on and let these forgotten treasures take you back in time to a world of passion, intrigue, and spectres both literal and symbolic. Be beguiled by tales of hauntings from Australia and beyond, and help us ensure that these talented writers don't become ghosts themselves.

Kathleen Jennings
4 May 2021

FROM SHADOW LAND, OR A TRAVELLER RETURNED

PUBLISHED IN THE SOUTH AUSTRALIAN
CHRONICLE ON 17 DECEMBER 1892.

JULIA S. HARRIS

1

'It harrows me with fear and wonder.'—Hamlet.

I HAD BEEN ENGAGED for some weeks with another detective in tracking a notorious criminal, the leader of a gang of coiners. He led us on a long chase, disappearing from one hiding place to another in a most marvellous manner. However, at last we captured our man, and feeling that I required a rest, I obtained leave of absence for a fortnight. On the same day, I ran down by the Great Western to Cheltenham, where my mother resided with my two younger sisters. So often when on duty, I had to travel by all sorts of conveyances at all hours of the day or night, that when off duty, I usually spent my holidays quietly at home. My mother and sisters were always glad to see me, and the change from the dust and grime of the slums of the East End, where I had spent the greater part of the last month, to the bright, pure air of the Cotswold Hills was very refreshing. My days were generally spent in rambling about this delightful neighbourhood, and in the evening, I pleased my mother and perhaps a friend or two by narrating my experience in the detection of crime in other parts of England. On returning one evening from one of my excursions, my mother put into my hand a note which on opening I found was from my cousin Dr Conway, who resided in Cambray. The note ran thus:

'Dear Ralph—If not engaged elsewhere, will you dine with me tomorrow evening at seven? Something has occurred that I wish to consult you about.

—Yours affectionately, Phil Conway.'

'Something has occurred,' I mused. 'Something important, too, or Phil would not require to consult me about it. One of those harebrained nephews of his in a scrape, I suppose. Just like them, always up to some mischief or another. Quite time Cicely came home and looked after them herself.' Having no other engagement, I decided to dine with Phil, so I sent a short note to him telling him to expect me at seven o'clock.

The next evening, a few minutes before seven, I sauntered down High Street and turned into Cambray. On reaching the house, I was surprised to see Phil watching for me. He let me in himself.

'The truth is,' he remarked apologetically as we entered the dining room, 'I have Cicely staying with me. She is very ill, suffering from a great shock to the nervous system. I am very anxious about her, and wish the house to be kept as quiet as possible.'

'Cicely!' I exclaimed. 'Where are the boys, then? I thought she had taken a house near Prestbury. She mentioned that she intended to do so last time I heard from her.'

'Yes, she did take a house, or rather I did for her, but a very unpleasant event occurred, and I thought it advisable to bring Cicely here till she found a suitable house. I have placed the boys for a term with one of the college masters, which I thought best under the circumstances.'

'Unpleasant event!' I repeated.

'Yes, a very unpleasant event,' Phil reiterated with emphasis, 'and that is what I wished to consult you about.'

Phil paused and looked keenly at me. I smiled at his earnestness.

'Nothing very horrible, I suppose,' I remarked lightly. 'Not attempted murder or anything of that kind.'

Phil's face grew longer.

'I really don't know,' he stammered. 'It might be even as serious as that, so don't laugh, Ralph. It is the appearance of a ghost to Cicely that has caused her illness.'

'A ghost?'

'Yes, a ghost. It must be a ghost,' he repeated as if to convince himself.

Knowing that till quite recently Phil had no belief in the supernatural, my first impulse was to laugh, but I controlled myself, as I was curious to know what had made such an impression on my usually matter-of-fact cousin.

'Well, tell me all about it, old man. It is a subject I am rather interested in. What kind of a ghost is it, and where is it to be seen?'

'I'm glad you take it so seriously, Ralph, for it is rather a long story that I have to tell you.'

Phil paused as if in doubt where to begin. 'You remember my telling you that I expected Cicely to return from Calcutta early in August, and that she had commissioned me to take a house for her in one of the suburbs and to have it furnished?'

I nodded.

'Well,' he continued, 'I met with a very prettily situated house, with a large garden attached, near Prestbury. There was a small coach house with a stable at the back of the garden. I decided in taking it, as Cicely had distinctly stated that should the house be any distance from town, she intended on keeping a pony phaeton. I gave the order to Sweeting for the furniture, choosing the greater part myself. When Cicely arrived, she was very much pleased with the house and grounds, and the boys, as you may imagine, were well pleased. Had they been allowed, the boys would have turned the stable into a rabbit hutch and the coach house into an aviary.'

I smiled, as I had a lively recollection of Phil's experience the two years that the boys had lived with him during their parents' absence in India. Good, easy Phil allowed them to do almost as they liked, the consequence being that the house was converted into a menagerie.

'About three weeks after Cicely took possession, I called to see her on my way to Prestbury. I did not think that she was looking very well, and told her so, when she pleaded a headache owing to the closeness of the weather. I was rather troubled about her and intended calling the next day, but being very busy neglected to do so. A few days after my visit, her eldest boy, Douglas, called on his way to school and told me that his mother had been very ill all night, and that old Martha wished me to come out at once. Questioning the boy, I learned that Martha had found their mother in an unconscious state on the drawing room floor, and that they had much trouble in restoring her. I was greatly alarmed at the news and drove out immediately to Gresham Lodge. I found Martha very anxious about her mistress, but she could give me no additional particulars, so I at once proceeded to Cicely's room. Her white, frightened face alarmed me, and as soon as I spoke, she burst into tears and begged me not to leave her. I saw at once that she was suffering from some great shock to the nervous system. She appeared totally unstrung and started nervously at the slightest sound. I questioned her as to the cause of her illness but could obtain no reply beyond an entreaty not to leave her, so I suggested that she should return with me and stay for a few days till she became better. She caught eagerly at my offer and begged me to take them all in till she could meet with another house, and I at once consented, as I saw something serious was the matter.'

'I did not question Cicely any further at the time, and it was some few days after, when she was more composed, that she told me the cause of her sudden illness. It seems that one evening after dark, she was standing at the head of the stairs, about to come down, when, to her surprise, she saw a young lady standing at the foot of the stairs. She wore an evening dress of black lace, in which was fastened a bouquet of crimson roses. Her hair, which was black, was coiled round her head and fastened with jewelled pins; handsome bracelets were on her arms, and her fingers sparkled with rings. The light from the hall lamp fell on her face, which was turned slightly upwards as if in the act of listening, and my sister was able to see that it was a very beautiful one. Her eyes, large and full, were fringed with long dark lashes, which gave a soft expression to her face, while her eyebrows were beautifully arched. Cicely was about to speak, but before she could do so the lady came swiftly up the stairs and entered the small room on the left of the landing, which Cicely had used as a box room. She did not appear to see my sister, though she passed close to her. Cicely, supposing the visit to be the result of a mistake, waited a few minutes, expecting to see the young lady return, but to her astonishment she heard the soft voice of the young lady speaking in a tone of passionate entreaty; the language was a foreign one, Cicely believes it to have been Spanish. The appeal, for appeal it appeared to be, continued for some minutes, then followed a bitter cry and the sound of a heavy fall. Terribly alarmed, Cicely rushed down the stairs and gave the alarm, "Someone in the box room!" Dawson, her groom, and the boys ran upstairs and thoroughly examined the room, but could find no one. Poor Cicely was very much upset by this experience, but did not say a word to anyone of what she had seen, though the boys were curious to know "how mother could have fancied anyone was in the box room".'

'One evening, exactly a week after this happened, Cicely was seated in the drawing room, reading, when she heard the door of the conservatory open. She looked up, expecting to see one of the boys, but instead the same young lady entered the room, whom she had met on the stairs. Cicely felt totally unable to speak or move. She says she would have given the world to have been able to call out, to break the horrible spell which seemed falling over her, but, dumb and speechless, she sat watching with beating heart the beautiful form of her visitor. The young lady did not appear to be aware of her presence, but swept up the long room with a gliding, graceful movement, and looked intently at the clock, which stood on the mantel shelf. Having apparently satisfied herself, she turned and walked to the opposite side of the room, to one of the mirrors hanging there, and gazed long and earnestly at her reflection. Cicely described it as a beautiful face; the large lustrous eyes, shaded by their long, dark lashes, were soft and sad. She had full pouting lips, a soft rounded chin, and a broad low forehead, with exquisitely arched eyebrows. As the lady gazed in the mirror, the expression of her face changed: her eyes filled with tears, and she wrung her hands as if in passionate grief. Suddenly, she raised her arms and unbound her hair, which fell in heavy masses below her knees. Then gathering it together again, she wound it round her head, hiding in its thick masses a small stiletto blade, which she drew from the folds of her dress. She still lingered in front of the mirror. When the clock struck eight, as the last stroke sounded through the room, she turned and walked towards the door. In doing so, she had to pass close to Cicely, of whose presence she still appeared to be perfectly unconscious. Cicely declares that as she passed her, she became aware of a peculiar sensation, which she describes as a breath of icy cold air blowing upon her. As the young lady left the room, Cicely must have fainted. You recollect that Martha found her in that state sometime after. On both occasions this happened on a Tuesday, so I determined to spend the following Tuesday evening at Gresham Lodge in order to see the young lady myself, if it were not a mere illusion of Cicely's, and if she really appeared, to ascertain if she were a somnambulist or indeed a spirit as Cicely believed.'

'Accordingly, the next Tuesday evening I drove to the Lodge shortly before eight o'clock, but unfortunately just as I was stepping out of the carriage, a gentleman I am acquainted with passed, and I was delayed a few minutes speaking to him. Entering by the front gate, I walked round to the back of the house, intending to enter by the conservatory door, of which I had the key. I was about to place the key in the lock when I experienced the cold, chilly feeling described by Cicely. Involuntarily looking behind me, I saw coming towards the door, from the direction of the coach house, a young lady dressed in black with a bouquet of crimson roses fastened in her dress, and otherwise answering to Cicely's description. I stepped quickly on one side to allow her to pass, which she did without appearing to see me, and then, opening the door—which I knew to be locked—without any apparent difficulty, she entered the house. I did not attempt to follow her into the house, but instead hurried back to the carriage and drove home. Now, Ralph, you have heard the story. What do you think of our experience, tell me candidly? Is this the spirit of a young lady who formerly resided at the Lodge, but who met with foul play and now returns to haunt the house, or have you some other theory?'

'Well, Phil,' I replied, 'to tell you the truth, I think that on further investigation, it will prove to be a somnambulist.'

'But,' objected Phil, 'the door. I am sure that it was locked.'

'Perhaps the young lady had a key to fit it.'

Phil looked disconcerted.

'But the fall, Ralph, and the strange feeling?'

'My idea is, Phil, that the young lady is a somnambulist, probably an actress. The foreign language might have been Italian, and the lady was rehearsing a tragic scene in her sleep. As to the feeling, that would be simply nervousness.'

Phil still looked dubious. 'I should like to ascertain the truth,' he persisted. 'Of course, if the young lady is a somnambulist, her visits to the house can be prevented and Cicely can return in peace, but I think we shall find it something more serious than that. I wish you would enquire into it, Ralph.'

Phil's emotion as he had related the experiences of his sister had aroused my curiosity respecting the young lady, so in response to his request, I readily promised to make a few enquiries, which I thought was all that would be necessary to clear up the mystery. I first enquired for the name and address of the owner of Gresham Lodge, and learned from Phil that the owner was Mr Gray, of Halifax House, Pittville, whom I had met before.

'All right,' I said, making a note of the address, 'I know Gray, he is a retired builder, a Yorkshire man, shrewd, and long-headed. Am I at liberty to repeat to him what you have told me?'

'Certainly, Ralph. I think we may trust Mr Gray. If he can give you the name and address of the last tenant, you might obtain some information from him that would be of assistance, but I have put the case in your hands now. I am sure you will be able to clear it up if anyone can. And now to dinner, Ralph, but say nothing of this to Cicely.'

2

'Lo you, here she comes! This is her very guise,
...Observe her; stand close.'—Macbeth.

AT BREAKFAST THE NEXT MORNING, I was very absent-minded, passing the salt for the sugar and making several other blunders to the amusement of my sisters, who made me generous offers for my thoughts. But I kept my own counsel, and shortly after nine o'clock, I made my way down Winchcombe Street towards Pittville. As I knocked at Mr Gray's door, it struck me that he would probably not take as great an interest in this business as did Phil or myself; indeed, he would not unlikely look upon it as a hoax. However, I had to risk his ridicule. I was shown into a handsomely furnished dining room by the servant, and Mr Gray was not long in making his appearance. I believe that the old gentleman was genuinely pleased to see me, for he gave me a most cordial welcome.

'I'm glad to see ye, lad, and how be ye gettin' on? Well, ye aren't wantin' me for anythin', be ye?' he asked, laughing at his own joke.

'No, Mr Gray, I don't want you for anything, but I wish you to give me a little information about the last tenant of Gresham Lodge. What was his name and his occupation?'

'I don't know nowt about him. I've only bought the house three months.'

I suppose my face showed my disappointment.

'What are it, lad?' he asked.

Without further preface I told Mr Gray of Dr Conway's unpleasant experience, and the still more unpleasant experience of his sister at Gresham Lodge. At first, he listened with a broad incredulous smile on his face, but as I described each scene he grew more and more interested, till, when I had finished my tale, he blurted out—

'I tell ye, ye and I and the doctor will go and meet the lady and see who her be, and I tell ye Mr Clarke of Pittville Street be the man I bought the house for; the last owner were a Mr Goldsborough.'

'All right,' I replied, greatly relieved at his taking my story so seriously, 'we will go tonight. Be there at half-past seven, and I will see Mr Clarke and perhaps will be able to ascertain something about it. At any rate, I shall look over the house and grounds during the day.'

'Do. I've been much taken with yer story, and I'm curious to see the endin'.'

I had no difficulty in finding Mr Clarke and after posing the same questions to him, elicited the reply that he had simply sold the house for a firm of solicitors, and knew nothing of the former tenant. Messrs Peabody & Sons, Montpelier were the solicitors; no doubt they would be able to give the information I desired.

Mr Peabody, senior, was absent on my arrival at his office, but I was able to see his son, whom I asked to oblige me with the name and present address of the last tenant of Gresham Lodge.

'The last tenant of Gresham Lodge?' he repeated, looking keenly —and I also thought suspiciously—at me. 'May I ask the reason of your enquiring?'

'I am making the enquiry for the present tenant, who has special reasons for wishing to see the last occupant, and I am referred to you by Mr Clarke, the house agent, who effected the sale of

Gresham Lodge for you, as the gentleman most likely to have the information I require.'

'We have no information respecting the last tenant,' replied Mr Peabody. 'The house was empty for two or three years, and we sold it for a gentleman who is now residing abroad.'

As I had no intention at this stage of taking this gentleman into my confidence, and it was evident that he did not intend to give me the information I wanted, I thanked him and withdrew, and, calling a cab, proceeded at once to Gresham Lodge in order to make a thorough examination of the house and grounds. I found that the grounds were surrounded by a high stone wall thickly set at the top with sharp, pointed pieces of glass. The house, an old-fashioned, comfortable villa residence, stood well back from the road; a tastefully laid out flower garden occupied the front; at the rear was a small orchard and vegetable garden, while to the right of this were a stable, coach house, and the usual outbuildings. I entered the house by the front door, which opened into a spacious hall. On the left of the hall were two doors communicating with the servants' apartments, and facing me was a handsome staircase, which after rising about six steps turned sharply to the right. On the right of the hall was a wide passage, in which were two doors. The first, about halfway down on the right, opened into the dining room. Here, nothing attracted my attention, and I did not delay, as it was not mentioned in Phil's story. The second was situated at the end of the passage, facing me as I walked down. This opened into the drawing room mentioned by my cousin, the room in which the young lady was said to appear. It was a long and rather narrow room, running the whole width of the house. At one end was a bow window overlooking the garden and commanding a distant view of the Cotswold Hills; at the other end of the room a stained-glass door opened into a small conservatory. This was the door through which the young lady was said to enter.

Passing through the conservatory, I made a careful examination of the grounds, coach house, stable, etcetera, but there also found nothing unusual or suspicious. The wall was apparently as firm as the day it was built: no loose stone or hole through which any person could enter in any part of it could I discover. How a lady could enter the grounds and appear coming from the direction of the coach house, as Phil had averred, I could not understand. However, I hoped to have the mystery cleared up shortly, and looked forward to the evening's meeting with increased curiosity.

Returning through the conservatory, I carefully locked the door, and before leaving the drawing room, made a few preparations for our visit in the evening. I put the clock right by my watch, set it going, and placed the lamps where they would throw a full light on the clock and mirror. Retracing my steps along the passage and across the hall, I walked upstairs to inspect the box room, which the young lady had entered, and where she was heard to speak for several minutes, and afterwards fall. This room was empty with the exception of a long row of bookshelves and a bookcase, which occupied the whole of one side of the room. Leaning on the mantel shelf as I looked round the room, I discovered that it was loose. I drew it carefully towards me, when, to my surprise, a small stiletto blade fell at my feet. As I picked it up, my heart gave a bound— there were blood stains on it. It was a very small weapon, with a richly chased handle, such as Spanish ladies often wear in their hair or carry concealed in their dress, and which they have been known to use at times with deadly effect in self-defence or when excited by jealousy and passion. But how came it here, in this house, near to a quiet English village? Whose blood had been spilt that now, after the lapse of several years, spoke so eloquently and more clearly than aught else of a tragedy that had been enacted? Yes, surely Phil's theory was correct. But, if so, what part did the young lady play in the tragedy? Was she sinned against or sinning? Did she recreate again her part in the tragedy when she was heard to cry and fall? I shuddered at the thought of what that part might be. Finding nothing more in the room to attract my attention, I now left the house and returned home to await our meeting in the evening.

Punctually at half-past seven o'clock, we met at Gresham Lodge. I could see that Phil was a trifle nervous, probably owing to his former experience, and Mr Gray looked serious, not to say awed. As for myself, after my find in the box room, I began to doubt my somnambulist theory and felt, I know not why, vaguely oppressed. I lighted the lamps in the hall and drawing room, and then seated myself by my friends in the bow window and watched anxiously for our expected visitor.

We were not disappointed. At a few minutes before eight o'clock, the door of the conservatory opened noiselessly and there entered a tall, beautiful girl with a lithe, graceful figure. She advanced rapidly up the room and stood for some seconds intently regarding the clock. While doing so, she was standing in the full glare of the lamps, and we were able to note her extreme beauty. Phil had described her accurately; her large soft dark eyes were sad, almost melancholy; the full pouting lips—a perfect Cupid's bow—were tremulous; in truth it was a sweet face, but at present sad with some great sorrow. Her black lace dress, which set off her clear, delicate complexion, was adorned with a bouquet of crimson roses: the only touch of colour that she wore.

Leaving the clock, she glided to one of the long mirrors on the opposite side of the room and gazed earnestly at her reflection there. As she looked, sorrow gave way to despair, and she wrung her hands as if in bitterest distress. Then, suddenly raising her arms, she drew the jewelled pins from her hair, letting it fall in heavy masses to her knees. Drawing from the folds of her dress a small stiletto, she wound it in her hair, which she re-coiled round her head, and with one long, lingering look in the mirror, she turned with a deep sigh and glided out of the room. With an almost superhuman effort, I rose and attempted to follow her. As I reached the door, the lady stood at the foot of the staircase in a listening attitude, as if in doubt. She then went swiftly up the stairs into the box room. As I followed, a soft voice in passionate entreaty fell on my ear and held me spellbound. But what she said I was not able to distinguish. Then followed a bitter cry, a heavy fall, and all was still.

I rushed up to the room—expecting to see I know not what—but found it empty, just as I had left it earlier in the day. My friends had not followed me, and when I returned to the drawing room, I found Phil administering a glass of brandy to Mr Gray, who appeared quite unnerved; Phil himself was also greatly agitated. To relieve the depression, I feigned a lightness I did not feel and rallied them on being so easily frightened, but they did not respond to my efforts, and we left the Lodge almost immediately to return home. As we neared Mr Gray's house, he broke the silence by exclaiming—

'Eh, the poor child, the poor child, I fear she have been cruelly treated. I wish I had nae bought the house!'

When we had parted with Mr Gray, I showed Phil the stiletto and informed him when and how I had found it. He was much impressed at this proof, as he considered it, of the correctness of his theory, and expressed himself as very confident that we should soon be able to discover why the young lady haunted the house.

3

'How now, Horatio! you tremble and look pale.
  Is not this something more than fantasy?
  What think you on't?'—Hamlet.

OUR EXPERIENCE at the Lodge determined me to prosecute a vigorous enquiry into the strange mystery, and if possible find the last tenant, whom I felt convinced was in some way connected with the young lady's appearance. Before retiring for the night, the thought occurred to me that perhaps the landlord of the village inn might be able to give me some information that would assist me in my search. I had lunched at the Pig and Whistle occasionally when walking in that direction, and found the host to be a chatty, garrulous fellow, well acquainted with the business of his neighbours and of the people for miles around. I decided to pay him another visit. The next morning, I walked out to the village of Prestbury, and, having ordered lunch at the inn, was soon engaged in a friendly chat with the landlord. I praised the neighbourhood and asked him if he knew of any house with eight or ten rooms with a good garden to let.

He rubbed his chin thoughtfully. 'I don't know if I does. There were a house, an' it were empty a good three years. Folks used to ask about it, but none could find out who had the lettin' on it. About six months ago it were advertised, an' it weren't long a'fore it were took.'

'What house was that?'

'That 'ere Gresham Lodge, about half a mile up the road. I 'ave a reason to remember it, for I were a bit sweet on the housemaid as lived there. A likely girl she were, she told me she were a'goin' away for a week to see her mother as lived in Gloucester, but she never come back. I ain't seen her since, an' that must be a good three year, for I married my missus two year come Michaelmas, an' it were a goodish while a'fore I took up with her.'

'What was her master's name?' I asked.

'I don't remember rightly, but I remember hers, it were Tilda Anne.'

'Was she a pretty girl?'

'Oh,' he answered, getting confidential, 'her were just that; my missis ain't a patch on her. Yellow curly hair an' blue eyes; as yellow as gold,' he added emphatically.

'I suppose you don't know anything about the people of the house?'

'No, we had something else to talk about, had Tilda an' me.'

'Did you know the young woman's surname?' I enquired.

'Did I know?' he repeated with a chuckle. 'Rather. It were Cook; Tilda Anne Cook. I'd like to know why her never come back,' he added reflectively.

I found the host ready enough to tell me all he knew about the residents of Gresham Lodge, but as he knew neither the name nor occupation of Tilda's master, his information was of little value, so after listening to a little more gossip I took my departure.

'Tilda Cook,' I repeated to myself as I walked home. 'I will advertise for you and try if I can induce you to come back, for you are the very person I want.'

Accordingly, I did advertise in both the local and the Gloucester papers that if Tilda Cook, who lived at Gresham Lodge near Prestbury three years ago, would apply to Ralph Grantly at Rodney Terrace, Cheltenham, she would hear of something to her advantage. Three days afterwards, I received a note purporting to come from Tilda's husband, she having changed her name during the last three years, telling me that he would call at Rodney Terrace that evening with his wife, whose present name was Appleby. The note was written most execrably and the spelling was equally bad, yet it was a long time since I had received a note that gave me as much pleasure. About seven o'clock the couple made their appearance, and I saw at once it was the right Tilda, for Mrs Appleby was as the landlord described her, and a very pretty young woman. The husband was a frank, straightforward-looking man a few years her senior. He was, she informed me, a coachman at Dr Cleasy's at Gloucester. I opened the conversation by saying that I wished to see her late master on business of great importance, and did she know where he was residing now. She replied that she did not; she had never seen or heard of him since Miss Carlotta had given her leave to visit her mother for a week. When she had been home three days, Mr Goldsborough, her master, had sent her a month's wages and told her that she need not return.

'Let me see,' I queried, 'Mr Goldsborough's Christian name was Ferdinand, was it not?'

'Yes, sir.'

'What relation was Miss Carlotta to him?'

'Well, sir, I don't rightly know, but I think she was his cousin. He always called her Carlotta, and she called him Ferdinand, but she was a foreign lady and used to talk to him a deal in her own language.'

'Was she young?'

'Lor' bless you, yes, sir. Not more than a year or two older than me. Master was a good deal older than her; nigh thirty he must have been an' she may be twenty. She were awful fond of him.'

'And he of her?' I queried.

'No, not like she were of him. He always spoke to her as if she were a child. He was always kind to her, but she just worshipped him. He was always trying to get her to go home. I often heard him talking to her about it. She was married, I found out. She had run away from her husband, but I did not find it out till the day a'fore she sent me home.'

'Married?' I exclaimed.

'Yes, sir, but don't you think bad on her, sir. She was a dear young lady and dreadful unhappy, for she told me once that master was the only one of her relations as was kind to her, and they was like brother and sister.'

'How did you find out that she was married?'

'Well, sir, it was like this. I was clearin' away the breakfast things and master was reading his letters. He got up an' gave one to Miss Carlotta, but she would not read it. She threw it in the fire. Master was vexed, and he said, "You are wrong, Carlotta, to treat your husband so. You should go home. You will lose your good name if you stay longer. He is willing and anxious to receive you." I was in the passage and heard her say, "Never, I will die first! Better die than live with him, the man I hate." And she threw herself on her knees and said something in her own language. I could tell she was begging him not to send her home.'

'What happened next?'

'I don't know. Master got up and shut the door.'

'Did they ever quarrel?'

'Never, sir. She were too fond of him, and he was always kind to her. He seemed sorry for her.'

'What was her surname?'

'Her what, sir?'

'Her married name?'

'I don't know, sir, I never heard her called anything but Miss Carlotta. Her clothes were marked "C.V.".'

'Should you recognise her if you were to see her?'

'Yes, sir. She was a tall, dark young lady with black hair; such hair you never saw, nigh down to her heels.'

'Would you object to go in company with your husband and myself tomorrow evening to Gresham Lodge to see a lady? We are anxious to know if she is Miss Carlotta. If you do so we will pay you well.'

'No, sir, I have no objection. I'd like to see Miss Carlotta again very much.'

'Very well, then, if your husband will call here tomorrow morning, I will make further arrangements with him for our visit to Gresham Lodge.'

'All right, sir,' Appleby answered. 'We ain't goin' back for a couple of days, as we thought we'd take a holiday. We'll call at eight tomorrow morning.'

Mr Appleby arrived punctually in the morning, and under promise of secrecy, I gave him the outline of this strange affair. I told him because I did not care to take the man's wife without his knowledge to a house that I believed to be haunted. I could see that the story made a painful impression on him, as he twisted his hat in his hands in a nervous frightened manner, but he could not resist the promised reward.

At the time agreed upon we met at the Lodge. I lighted the lamps as before and tried to give a cheerful air to the room, but in spite of my efforts there was something eerie about it.

At the usual time, the tall, dark figure of the young lady glided up the room. As she did so, I looked at Mrs Appleby. Her lips were parted in a pleased smile of recognition, and she appeared as glad to see her former mistress as she had said she would be. The lady looked and acted precisely as she had done on the occasions when we had seen her before. As she gazed at her reflection in the mirror and wrung her hands in bitter despair, great tears welled from the eyes of her humble friend by my side, and the despair on one face was visibly reflected on the other. As the lady crossed the room to reach the door, she appeared to glance in our direction, and, to my surprise, instead of immediately leaving the room as before, she stood at the unopened door, gazing with a look of sad entreaty at the woman by my side. Mrs Appleby had become much agitated and, as the lady approached us, rose and was about to speak to her, but was restrained by her husband, who was scarcely less agitated. Sitting down again, she appeared to suddenly become aware that what she saw was not Miss Carlotta in the flesh, but her spirit, and as she realised this she turned deadly pale and fell in a swoon at our feet.

The strokes of the clock vibrating through the room seemed to break the spell. The young lady glided into the passage and disappeared.

I did not attempt to follow her or listen for the sounds that I knew would be heard—the dreadful ending to each of her visits—but followed Appleby, who had raised his wife in his arms and rushed through the open door of the conservatory. He did not stop till he reached the front gates—which I unlocked—and, hailing a cab, drove to Phil's house at Cambray. Mrs Appleby was some time before she recovered consciousness, when she told us with a rush of tears that it was indeed Miss Carlotta whom we had seen.

Appleby told me afterwards that 'I would not go there again, not for a hundred pounds; it had so upset my missus'.

I pieced together the information I had received and came to the conclusion that the lady was a relative of Mr Goldsborough, who was the last tenant as well as owner of Gresham Lodge. That she was a spirit I was also assured. Her look of piteous entreaty on my last visit filled me with a desire to learn her history. Could it be that a dreadful tragedy had been enacted here? Mrs Appleby was sure that she was married. Had she met her death by the hands of a revengeful husband? The bloodstained stiletto pointed to that. The abrupt dismissal of Mrs Appleby from their service, the family's removal from the neighbourhood, the house standing so long untenanted, Mr Peabody's refusal to give me the last tenant's name:

these were all suspicious circumstances and pointed to Mr Goldsborough being implicated.

I determined to again visit Messrs Peabody on the morrow, as I felt certain that when I produced the bloodstained stiletto and told them the suspicions that had been aroused, Mr Goldsborough's lawyers would see the propriety of satisfying my enquiries, if by doing so a scandal could be avoided.

4

'Alas, poor ghost!'—Hamlet.

THE NEXT MORNING I called on Messrs Peabody & Sons and was fortunate enough on this occasion to find the senior partner within, willing to grant me an interview. Considering that nothing was to be gained by beating about the bush, I at once stated the nature of my business and our suspicions respecting the former tenants of Gresham Lodge, watching Mr Peabody narrowly as I did so. I related at length the particulars of the young lady's appearances, dwelling on the strange action of her hiding the stiletto in her hair, and also pointed out to him how impossible it was for any person to reside in a house haunted by this most unhappy young lady. It seemed to me impossible to doubt that a terrible tragedy had occurred at the Lodge, and that his client, Mr Goldsborough, had played some part in it. I had called on him, I said, believing that he was in a position to give me the information necessary to clear up the mystery. If he would do so, and could give me a satisfactory explanation of the appearances and behaviour of the young lady, I could assure him I had no wish or intention to cause any annoyance to his client. But if, as on the former occasion when I had seen his son, he still declined to give me any information—well, I reminded him that I had obtained the information in my possession without their assistance and, being a detective by profession, would no doubt be able to follow up the clue I had found, and if any crime had been committed, bring the offenders to justice. The appearance and behaviour of the young lady had made such an impression on the several persons who had seen her that they were determined to sift the matter to the bottom and ascertain if she had met with foul play, that she thus haunted the house exhibiting such distress.

'Has this apparition been undoubtedly recognised by any person? Do you suspect Mr Goldsborough of foul play merely because a ghost appears in a house once owned by him?'

I told Mr Peabody that a former servant there, Tilda Anne Cook, now Mrs Appleby, had recognised the young lady as Miss Carlotta, a cousin of Mr Goldsborough, who had lived at Gresham Lodge with him when she was a servant there, and I ended by laying the bloodstained stiletto on the table.

At the sight of the stiletto, Mr Peabody gave an involuntary start, and his face underwent a great change; the assumed indifference rapidly gave place to sorrow, and he was deeply moved. Rising from his chair, he carefully locked the door of the room, then turning to an iron safe which stood in a corner, he took from the top shelf a small brown tin box which had the letters 'F.C.G.' painted on it.

'I have here,' he said, unlocking the box and turning to me, 'what I think will not only convince you of the innocence of Ferdinand Goldsborough, but also enlist your sympathy. But if when you have read this you are not satisfied, I will give you his present address, then you will be able to see him yourself. I must first tell you that Ferdinand Goldsborough is the son of a very dear friend of my own. Ferdinand's father was a very unfortunate man— unfortunate in everything, even in his marriage, for he married a domineering Spanish lady: a proud, handsome woman who married poor Rupert for his money and position, for he had both when he married her. She led him such a life that the poor fellow looked upon it as a positive blessing when she left him and returned to her relatives at Valparaiso, which she did not do till she had almost ruined him with her extravagance. Ferdinand's early life was spent in this town, but then as he neared manhood his father died insolvent, and it became necessary for Ferdinand to maintain himself. His mother, who resided with her cousin at Valparaiso, sent for him, having heard of her husband's death, and offered him a post in her cousin's office. As it seemed a good offer, I advised Ferdinand to accept it. Many times since, I have regretted giving him that advice. But who can see into the future? He was away ten years when a bachelor brother of his father died and left him all his property, Gresham Lodge being part of it. On receiving news of the legacy, he at once returned to England, intending to remain here. After transacting some necessary business in London, he took up his residence at Gresham Lodge. What happened from that time to the date of that dreadful catastrophe is written down here, signed by Ferdinand Goldsborough and witnessed by me.'

He handed me as he spoke a closely written manuscript.

'Read it,' he continued, 'and you will understand what is now a mystery to you.'

I opened the document, which was written in a firm hand, and read as follows:

I, Ferdinand Goldsborough, do hereby solemnly declare that what I am about to relate is the true version of that most unhappy event which happened at Gresham Lodge in the month of October, 186—.

To make the circumstances clear, I must go back a few years in my history, to the time when I lived in my cousin's house at Valparaiso.

Xavier Verco was the son of my mother's uncle, at whose house my mother had been brought up from her infancy, so that when she left England, she returned there as a matter of course, and, on my arrival at Valparaiso after my father's death, he received me with the greatest kindness and has in all ways proved himself my friend.

It was in the year 1865 that Xavier, then a man of sixty, became deeply enamoured of the young daughter of Joseph Perdita, his business partner. She had just returned from a convent school and was a mere child in both feelings and ideas. I was at the time away at Santiago on business and was much surprised on hearing the news of the intended marriage from my mother, who was herself much annoyed at what she termed Xavier's folly. At her father's bidding, her tastes and wishes not being considered in the least, the beautiful Carlotta Perdita married the rich merchant, Xavier Verco, and became his wife.

After the wedding, I still continued to reside with my mother at my cousin Xavier's, as I could not persuade her to occupy a separate house with me. Carlotta was so young and inexperienced, she said, quite unable to manage so large a house. Carlotta's sweetness and gentleness of disposition endeared her to all who knew her, except my mother, who regarded Carlotta as an interloper, and taking advantage of her youth, would have treated her unkindly, even harshly, had I not shielded her by my presence.

Under these circumstances we soon became much attached to each other. I regarded Carlotta as a very dear sister—I swear she was nothing more—but, as I learned afterwards, she regarded me with much warmer feelings, and this was the beginning of the trouble.

It was about two years after this marriage that a near relative of my father died and bequeathed to me considerable property, which rendered it necessary for me to proceed to England on a lengthy visit. I began to make preparation for my departure, and one day when I was alone with Carlotta, I remarked that I should soon have to say goodbye. She shrugged her shoulders petulantly and exclaimed, 'Do not speak of it. When do you return?' 'Perhaps never, Carlotta,' I replied. 'My mother thinks that I should marry now that I have ample means. Perhaps I may do so in England.'

To my surprise she became greatly excited. 'Never, Ferdinand, you must not; you shall not be so cruel! What, leave me, your poor Carlotta? I could not bear it; I should die; my heart would break. Say you do not mean it, Ferdinand, say you do but jest.'

She threw herself on her knees and clasped my hand. I tried to quiet and soothe her, for I was fearful lest some eavesdropper should hear her passionate unguarded language and work harm to the excited girl. 'Listen, Ferdinand; take me with you; I will be your sister, but do not leave me here.'

I reminded her of her husband and begged her to remember his honour, but she sprang to her feet, her eyes blazing with anger. 'Remember my husband?' she hissed. 'Yes, I will remember him. He bought me from my father for $20,000. My father sold me, I tell you; I know it. My husband was angry one day and he said to my father, "I gave you $20,000 when I married your daughter; I will not give you any more." They were quarrelling and did not hear me enter. I came between them and I said to my father, "Is it true? Did this man pay $20,000 for me? Is it true that you sold me? Lie not to me or I will kill you." He said, "Leave the room, Carlotta. This is no place for you." "This is my house," I said, "the house you sold me to. I will not leave the room. Tell me the truth." But he would not speak. Then I turned to my husband, "Will you tell me the truth?" I said. "Did you give my father $20,000 for me?" and he said "Yes, it is true." Then I said to my father, "I give you as many curses as you received dollars for me. You shall never come to my house again; never".

'I am a slave, I tell you, Ferdinand. I was bought—bought,' she exclaimed bitterly, 'just as they buy slaves. Ferdinand, pity me, I am only nineteen and a slave for life. I cannot buy my freedom; I can only break my chains. Pity me, Ferdinand, and take me with you; I ask no more.'

I was greatly shocked at Carlotta's passionate outbreak, and if possible, more so at the cause of it, though I knew how little the feelings of the daughter were considered in these marriages. 'Carlotta,' I said, 'when did this happen?' 'Last week,' she replied laconically, exhausted by her passion.

I talked long and earnestly with Carlotta, telling her that she would always be dear to me as a sister and that I would always protect her, as I had done in the past. I promised her that I would return again as soon as I had transacted my business in England, but all to no avail. 'If you will not take me with you I will go by myself,' she reiterated.

Three days after this scene I sailed alone. Carlotta was not visible when I left the house, and I felt it would be cruel to ask for her. She told me afterwards that my mother had overheard our conversation and had locked her in her room to prevent her accompanying me. However, I knew nothing of this at the time.

About six weeks after I had taken up my residence at Gresham Lodge, my housekeeper told me that a lady wished to see me. To my surprise, I found Carlotta seated in the drawing room. 'Ferdinand,' she exclaimed excitedly, 'I have come.' 'So I see, Carlotta,' I answered gravely. 'Do not be solemn, my dear cousin. I could not stay; I have broken my chains.' 'Carlotta,' I said, 'listen to me. I shall at once write and acquaint your husband of your arrival here. I, at least, will take care of your good name, which you have perilled so rashly.' 'Good name?' she said scornfully. 'You forget I have been bought, like a bale of merchandise, from Joseph Perdita. I do not care one pin for what you call my good name. I will not be the wife of Xavier Verco anymore. I will be free. If you turn me out—well, I will live elsewhere, but I will never return. Your mother drives me mad, and I hate it all.'

I knew Carlotta was quite capable of doing as she threatened, and I did not dare to let so beautiful a girl go away to reside amongst strangers, so I reluctantly consented to her staying in my house. However, I told her that by the outgoing mail I should write to her husband and tell him of her arrival, as I considered it would be unjust to him and to her not to do so. 'Do as you will and tell him I will never return—never! I will never be his wife again! I hate him!' she answered passionately.

I did not attempt to argue with her, as I knew it was useless when she was in one of her wilful passionate moods, so I let her have her own way. I called my housekeeper and informed her that the lady was my cousin and a foreigner, that as she could speak but very little English, I wished her to look after her comfort. She was a worthy woman and she looked dubiously at Carlotta; her extreme beauty appeared to make her suspicious, but that soon wore off, and she became very much attached to her young mistress.

As I had promised, by the next outgoing mail I wrote to my mother and Carlotta's husband informing them of her arrival and that she was now staying at Gresham Lodge under the care of my housekeeper. As soon as it was possible for a reply to reach England, we heard from both. My mother, as we expected, was furiously angry and used numberless threats to both of us. Xavier wrote to me, enclosing a letter to Carlotta. He informed me that he exonerated me from blame and still trusted my honour. To Carlotta he wrote entreating her to return, promising if she would that he would forgive and forget all. I added my entreaty to that of her husband, but it was to no avail. Carlotta had decided to remain, and she did so.

For several months we lived together. With the exception of occasional fits of depression, Carlotta appeared to be happy. One morning about six months after Carlotta arrived, I received a letter from my mother, in which she stated that she had determined to take the next steamer to England, accompanied by her servant Pedro, and that, if necessary, she would employ force to compel Carlotta to return home with her. When I showed this letter to Carlotta it roused her warm passionate nature to a furious heat. 'I will never return alive,' she exclaimed, 'your mother is a bad woman. Why does she interfere with me? And Pedro,' she shuddered. 'I hate and fear that man. I always feel as if he were a snake; he always watched me. He is your brother's servant and he is her slave. If she said, "Pedro, kill Carlotta," he would do it.'

About a week after this, Carlotta told me that she had given Mrs Todd, the housekeeper, a week's holiday, and a few days later the housemaid was missing. I asked Carlotta where she was. 'Matilda will return this evening,' Carlotta answered. I told her she was foolish to give this servant a holiday till the housekeeper returned. That evening about eight, I returned from town and, letting myself in with a latchkey, went straight to my study. A few minutes afterwards, I heard a timid knock at the door and Carlotta entered. Before I could speak, she burst into a fit of tears and begged me to defend her from my mother. 'Ferdinand, take me from the man I hate; take me, let me be yours. There must be a law to free me from him. I am not his wife; I am his slave. I have been bought. You say slaves are free here; make me free. Ferdinand, let me be your wife. Do not turn from me. I have loved you always—always, though you did not know it. Ferdinand, have pity on me.'

She poured out such a flood of passionate entreaty that I was utterly bewildered and knew not what to do or say. Indeed, I felt so keenly for her in her distress that I hardly dared look at her tearful face lest my resolution for her good would fail. 'Carlotta,' I begged, 'my poor ill-used girl, say no more. It cannot be. It is impossible.'

In my despair of convincing her that I was powerless to free her from her chains, I feigned a love I did not feel for a young lady whom we had met several times since her arrival in England. 'Is it true, Ferdinand? Say it is not true.' 'It is true, Carlotta.'

O fatal falsehood! Would that I had been dumb. 'Then die,' she exclaimed, and drawing swiftly from her hair a glittering stiletto, she struck at my heart. When I saw what Carlotta intended, I threw myself backward in order to avoid the blow.

This would not have saved me, but fortunately I had my purse in my breast coat pocket, and as the point of the stiletto pierced this, it was stopped by a florin. The force of the blow caused me to stumble and fall. Carlotta, seeing this and thinking she had killed me, plunged the stiletto into her own breast with a cry of despair, falling to the floor bleeding. As soon as I regained my footing, I sprang to her assistance, but it was too late; she was beyond human help. In a few moments, she breathed her last in my arms. I believe the stiletto had pierced her heart.

Picture my horror, my despair at that moment. I would have given all I had, even my life, could I have recalled the words that had caused this dreadful catastrophe, but it was too late; the spirit of the beautiful Carlotta had fled, and I was alone with the dead.

What was I to do? What course should I take? What punishment would the law mete out to me if I were found in such a position, alone in the house with the dead body of this beautiful girl? A loud knock at the door startled me. I ran downstairs and opened it expecting to see the housekeeper returned, but it was a messenger with a telegram from my mother. She had landed at Southampton and would be with me tomorrow.

The morrow came, and with it my mother, Donna Goldsborough, as she persisted in calling herself. My pale, agitated face told her something was amiss. 'Where is Carlotta?' she enquired. 'Come and see,' I replied. I took her to my study where the poor girl lay. Standing beside Carlotta's lifeless form, I told my mother all. No sorrow or compunction was visible on her hard, handsome face. 'God,' she exclaimed, 'she could not have done better. It is well. Xavier is free, and so art thou. Leave thy Madre and Pedro. We will have no scandal. The church has no prayers for such as she. We will bury her this night in the garden, and thou shalt return with me. I have said it. Go,' she added imperiously.

I had been so long accustomed to give way to my mother's haughty, imperious will that I obeyed, and being worn out by the terrible anguish of the past night, I threw myself on my bed dressed as I was. When I awoke, it was past midnight and the moon was shining in at the open window, throwing strange shadows across the room. With an effort I recalled the events of the past day. Seeing the open window, I rose to close it. As I did, my ears caught the sound of a muffled thud as of someone digging. My mother's words flashed through my mind. They were digging Carlotta's grave. I crept quietly downstairs and out of the back door, keeping well in the shade of the trees till I reached the coach house, under the shelter of which I stood. Standing there I watched Pedro's movements. How I loathed the man, for, like Carlotta, I believed him capable of any villainy. He was digging a grave under the large lilac bush, the branches of which he had tied well back. A few minutes later I heard my mother's voice in a shrill whisper, 'Haste, Pedro; he will waken; the day will soon break.'

A muttered '*Diable*' was the only answer from Pedro, as he straightened himself and shook the earth from his clothes. Climbing up out of the grave he had dug, he joined my mother, who stood under the shade of a large pear tree. '*Chut!*' I heard her say contemptuously as Pedro raised in his arms a roughly constructed coffin and staggered with it to the open grave. With a great effort, I restrained myself from rushing out. For that wretch to touch poor Carlotta's remains seemed sacrilege to me. He placed the coffin on a board and slid it to its last resting place. 'Ugh,' he grunted, 'I like not the work.' 'Be not a fool,' said my mother sharply. 'Hasten with thy work; quick, the time flies.'

Pedro had been too accustomed to obey his imperious mistress to rebel now. He hastily filled in the grave, and untying the branches of the lilac bush, allowed them to spring back into their accustomed place. The fragrant shrub well hid the dreadful secret.

I made my way quickly back to the house and threw myself on the bed, but not to sleep; my brain was too excited and my heart too sore. I could not banish from my thoughts the scene I had witnessed. As the morning dawned, my mother entered the room, bringing me a cup of coffee. She looked very suspiciously at me when she observed I had not undressed. She had evidently desired to hide from me the exact place of Carlotta's burial. 'I like not this heathen land,' she remarked as I drank the coffee. 'We will return soon. Thou canst make the arrangements.' 'Carlotta?' I asked. Her brow darkened. 'The dead is buried; ask no more.'

The next day, I called on my father's old friend, Mr Peabody, and told him the above facts, which he desired me to put into writing. I also left with him the purse with the florin.

FERDINAND COSTELLO GOLDSBOROUGH.

Witness—H. C. Peabody.

As I placed the manuscript on the table, Mr Peabody broke the silence.

'This is the purse mentioned,' he said, 'examine it.'

On examining the purse, I found it had been pierced on one side by some sharp instrument. Trying the stiletto, I found it fit the spot exactly, striking against the florin, which the purse still contained.

'Now that you have read that statement,' said Mr Peabody, 'do you consider that any good purpose would be served by exposing an honourable man before the eyes of a gaping, horror-loving public?'

'No, Mr Peabody,' I replied, 'I do not. I should be very reluctant to cause any additional pain to Mr Goldsborough, but I consider that he should repurchase the house from Mr Gray. It is impossible for anyone to occupy a house thus haunted by the spirit of this most unhappy young lady.'

'Mr Goldsborough will do so at once, I am sure. We were not aware of this peculiarity when we sold it.'

'Did Mr Goldsborough's mother return to Valparaiso?' I enquired.

'Yes, and married Xavier Verco, whom she rules with a rod of iron.'

'And Mr Goldsborough?'

'Mr Goldsborough did not return with his mother. The associations of the lodge were too unpleasant for him to continue to reside there. For a short time he rented another house, but the climate of England did not suit him. After ten years' residence in the warm, sunny clime of Chile, he found our winter weather too bleak and cold, so he returned. He now resides in Santiago, but he refuses to hold any communication whatsoever with his mother. He regards her as morally responsible for Carlotta's death.'

About three months after my interview with Mr Peabody, I received a letter from Mr Goldsborough, dated from Santiago. He thanked us warmly for our consideration and kindness to him in not making our discovery at Gresham Lodge public and informed us that if he had known of Carlotta's visits, nothing would have induced him to sell the house. Instead, he should now close it up; it should be sacred to her. So, we feel assured that during the lifetime of Ferdinand Goldsborough, that sad spirit from shadowland will never be again disturbed by mortal visitors.

JULIA S. HARRIS

Dates of Birth and Death—Unknown | Published from 1891-1897.

The elusive Julia S. Harris is as ghostly as her writing—like many talented women authors, she has almost completely disappeared from the written record. Harris owned her status as a woman writer within Adelaide's writing community by often adopting the pen name 'Mrs Robert Harris'; while other evidence of her life has been lost to time, her pen name reveals to us that she was the wife of a Robert Harris. She was also the mother of an Elizabeth Fortesque, who passed away at just five months old. She likely helped to support her family with the money she made from small writing prizes, such as the *Western Mail's* Christmas story competition, translating the tragedy of her personal life into stories of murder, betrayal, and doomed romance. Such serialised works, including "The Oakhurst Tragedy" and "Sir Jaspar's Ward, or The Wraith of Trevor Park", were published in *The Adelaide Observer*, *The South Australian Chronicle*, the *Western Mail*, and *The Healesville Guardian*. In another of her works, "Euphemia Redmond: The

Guardian Spirit of Knockmey Hall", Harris included the epigraph from poet Henry Wadsworth Longfellow:

All houses in which men have lived and died
Are haunted houses.

Such a sentiment is echoed in Harris' oeuvre, as she uses the symbolic haunted house to interrogate aspects of Australian culture that remain relevant to her contemporaries. Many of Harris' stories explore the sinister histories of gendered violence, xenophobia, and class discrimination that lurk behind the stately English manor. Her work may be interpreted as an Australian's critique or rejection of a culture inherited from our colonial predecessors.

Corella Press is proud to restore Harris' unique voice to Australian literary history.

A MAN AND HIS MONEY

PUBLISHED IN THE DAILY NEWS FROM 30
SEPTEMBER TO 16 OCTOBER 1899

JENNY WREN

1

FAY CALDERON's life had undergone a great change. Once the petted child of her father—feted, admired, a veritable queen in her own county—she was now a despised, ignored governess with no salary but her board and lodging.

For when Colonel Calderon died, it was found that he had been living beyond his means and that there was not a penny left for his daughter.

So Fay caught at the chance a distant relative of her father's offered her, and she came to Brookside Manor to teach Mrs Renton's younger daughter. But the life was intolerable to her, and the more she saw of the family, the more she disliked it.

Henry Renton, the master of the house, never took any notice of her. He was a solicitor and had no thought or feeling about anything in the world but:

'Gold, gold, gold;
Hard and bitter and cold.'

He was very well-off, but he hoped to be better still one day, for an old cousin of his who lived at Brookside and who was known to be rich, had no relations to leave his money to except the solicitor and his brother Charles, who had a small vicarage in the South of England.

And Old Pete Renton was also supposed to be a miser, for he lived in a small place called the Yews—on account of the dark, sinister-looking trees which formed an avenue up to the house. He never went outside his own domain, nor did he ever receive a visitor, and, try as he might, Henry Renton could never gain admittance. The old man lived alone with an old housekeeper, and it was the latter of whom the solicitor was chiefly afraid. Supposing she should influence his cousin and induce him to leave her all his money!

Henry Renton had three children: a son, Philip, an uncouth, gauche-looking man; Fay Calderon's pupil, Ethel; and his elder daughter, Maud, who had reached the age of twenty-seven, and, to the great disappointment of herself and her mother, still remained unmarried.

Maud was furiously jealous of Fay's charming face and lovely voice. When she found how much the governess was admired, she got her mother to banish her to the schoolroom and only allow her to appear at the breakfast table.

But one day, a sudden shock disturbed the equilibrium of the Manor. The news reached it that Old Pete Renton, the miser, was dead.

The solicitor became terribly excited in a moment. He went over to the Yews, assumed possession at once, saw to all the funeral arrangements, and wired to his brother Charles to come up to attend it.

Charles was very different to Henry. He was a studious man, and his heart was absolutely wrapped up in his only child, Captain Renton. In fact, he would have only welcomed any money for his son Rex's sake.

However, he looked around the study at the Yews with a sigh when, after the funeral, he followed his brother's family and the solicitor into the dead man's house to hear the reading of the will.

The walls were lined with books his heart had often longed for in vain. What was to become of these priceless treasures?

The old housekeeper, Rebecca, stood in the corner, but she seemed like a stone, unconscious of everything that went on around her. Yet there were no tears. She only stared straight in front of her, but with such a grief-stricken look that Fay Calderon's heart ached as she saw her.

Mr Brand, Old Pete's solicitor, took up the will, cleared his throat, and began. Divested of its legal habiliments, the text ran as follows:

'To Rebecca Grey I leave'—Henry raised his eyes and scowled across at the old woman. He dreaded to hear the next words. Was she to have all?—'£200 a year and the cottage called the Glen, on the cliff beyond the Brookside Woods, to dispose of as she pleases after her death. I ask my cousins to take care of her and see that she requires nothing as long as she lives.'

Henry Renton took out his handkerchief and mopped his brow. The relief was almost too much for him. Only the Glen and £200 a year! He could have laughed aloud with pleasure.

Fay again looked across at Rebecca, to see if the news had moved her in any way, but the old woman seemed scarcely to have heard. In all likelihood, thought the girl, she knew about it before.

'I desire that the Yews,' went on Mr Brand, 'should be sold, and the proceeds divided between my two cousins, Henry and Charles Renton.'

Henry gave a contemptuous snort.

'Pete was generous!' he said with an uneasy laugh. 'I can't imagine anyone giving £10 for this rickety hole!'

Mr Brand frowned. He did not care for interruptions.

'All my books and my manuscripts,' he continued, 'I leave to my cousin, Charles Renton.'

The vicar's face fairly shone with delight.

'All his books? I am to have all these books—these rare volumes that I see now on the shelves!' he cried in a voice of ecstasy, scarcely daring to believe his fortune.

'Oh, go on! Go on!' cried Henry impatiently, not to say rudely. His hopes were raised tenfold by the news of Charles's legacy. Surely the rest of the money—Old Pete's whole fortune—must come to him? There was no one left now who had any claim besides himself.

Mr Brand pursed up his lips at the tone, and—perhaps out of the perversity of his nature, and because he saw the excitement of the other—his words came very slowly from his lips.

'And the rest of my fortune, amounting to £80,000, I leave absolutely to——'

Here Mr Brand paused with dramatic effect and enjoyed the excitement depicted on the faces around him. A breathless silence prevailed.

'Go on, for goodness' sake!' gasped Henry Renton.

'I leave absolutely to anyone who can find it! Be they kin or stranger, friend or alien, the person who finds the £80,000 shall have it for his or her life and dispose of it as he or she pleases after death.'

There was silence in the old library for at least two minutes after Mr Brand had finished, then a loud oath rang out from Henry Renton's lips.

'What a will!' he cried, his face ashy pale, and his voice hoarse with anger. 'What an iniquitous will! Of course, it can never stand for a moment!' And he gave a harsh, mirthless laugh. 'It is the will of a madman—hopelessly, helplessly mad! I will dispute it! I would not allow such a will to stand for a moment!'

The corners of Mr Brand's mouth curled upwards—the only attempt at a smile in which he ever allowed himself to indulge.

'If you mean to dispute the will on the plea of the insanity of my client,' he broke in distinctly, 'I am afraid you will not have much of a case—nay, rather, any person who suggested that the author of "Treatises of the Soul" was mad would be looked on as insane himself.'

The vicar started, and his eyes turned from the volumes, which they had been regarding with all the joy of possession.

'"Treatises of the Soul"?' he said quickly. 'Why, they are by that great writer "Hermit".'

'Quite correct,' answered Mr Brand suavely. 'They were written by "Hermit", alias Mr Peter Renton, my client.'

'But "Hermit" is one of the greatest philosophers of the day!' cried Charles Renton.

'Quite correct,' repeated Mr Brand. 'The world of science has lost a great leader in my client.'

The vicar sat down again, with a feeling of awe and yet pride in that he had been related to so great a man. But his brother's anger was growing with every minute. He felt he had been villainously dealt with. Oh, that money! If he could only find it! His eyes swept the room, and, in doing so, fell on the bent figure of Rebecca.

He strode up to her.

'Old woman,' he cried, 'this is your doing! You know where this money is hidden! Give it up!'

Rebecca looked up at him half-dazed and began muttering words unintelligible to him.

'Bah!' he cried with another oath, turning away from her vacant eyes. 'She is mad too—they are all mad! But in spite of Old Pete and her,' he muttered furiously between his teeth, 'in spite of everyone, I will get that money yet!'

Rebecca got up as he moved away and went in the direction of the door, but her steps were so feeble, and she trembled so that she would have fallen, had not Fay flown to her assistance and helped her as she stumbled out of the room.

'You will get into trouble, young woman,' whispered Philip Renton, as Fay went back to her seat. He shot a glance in his father's direction.

But Fay only shrugged her shoulders contemptuously.

'What do I care?' she said, with a laugh. 'I am not afraid of Mr

Renton!' She always scorned Philip for the abject fear in which he held his father.

But Henry Renton was too busy thinking of other things to take any notice of Fay's action.

'It must be in this house,' he conjectured, 'or buried in the garden grounds. And it is to be sold. Come what may—if the price runs into tens of thousands—I will buy it! Yes, even if I have to ruin myself to do it!'

The Yews had gone up in Mr Renton's estimation during the last half hour.

2

MATTERS DID NOT IMPROVE at the Manor after Old Pete's death. During the time that elapsed between the funeral and the sale of the Yews, Henry Renton was literally unapproachable. His restlessness and his irritability, resulting as they did from suppressed excitement, found full vent on his wife and family, with the result that every member of the household fled at the sound of his footstep.

He chafed at the necessary delay and feared that the probability of hidden treasure might get abroad and the value of the little broken-down house rise to such a pitch that he would be beaten out of the field. It grew to be a fixed idea—the sole and supreme aim of his life—that he should obtain possession of Old Pete's money.

Though it was not on account of the hidden treasure, Henry Renton found a powerful antagonist in the field when the auction day arrived. For a rich American had lately bought property in the neighbourhood, and it just happened that the acre on which the Yews stood had become very necessary in his eyes.

Consequently, the men bid against each other until the price grew into large figures. When at last it was knocked down to Renton, the man was staggered to think how far he had gone.

He mopped his face in the way he had when he grew at all excited, and wondered how he had dared to risk so much money. But the fact that he had been successful soon sent all other matters out of his head, and he began to comfort himself with the idea that, fortunately, half the amount he had paid would come back to him through the provision in Old Pete's will. When he had found what he wanted, he could sell the place to the American at his own price and make a nice little fortune out of the matter.

After all, why should he worry about such a paltry amount when he was so certain now to become the possessor of £80,000 in such a very little time?

He came home jubilant and called his wife into his study to tell her of his success. But Mrs Renton was not so optimistic in her views as her husband, and nothing could make her think of the purchase of the Yews in any other way than that of an iniquitous expenditure.

'Now you have spent all your capital,' she exclaimed. 'We have nothing to live on but what you make, and that is in no way a certain means of subsistence.'

'I tell you,' answered Henry, growing angry, 'that I will get half the money back, and the rest goes to Charles! He may thank his stars for the amount that little hovel fetched! I don't suppose it will be very long before the £80,000 turns up.'

'Supposing the £80,000 is not at the Yews at all?' thought his wife with a sigh as she turned away. But she dared not suggest such a contingency to her husband.

'My charming family is in such a delightful temper tonight that I simply can't stay downstairs any longer,' said Philip Renton that same evening, lounging into the schoolroom where Fay was sitting by herself, playing little snatches of tunes upon the cottage piano.

He had got into the habit of coming upstairs lately and keeping Fay company, and he was a visitor Miss Calderon in no way appreciated. She would far rather have been left alone with her music. Besides, lately his manner had undergone a change that annoyed her, for his voice had adopted a familiarity in tone which fairly disgusted her.

She took no notice of his entrance now but continued to run her fingers lightly over the piano, so Philip threw himself into a chair by her side with a sigh of content.

'It's peaceful here, at any rate,' he said. 'There's no nagging in Queen Fay's kingdom! It was a good slice of luck for you,' he went on, as Miss Calderon disdained to answer, 'being banished up here, away from the storms and frictions downstairs. There's Maud, who can't speak an amiable word to a fellow!'

Fay raised her little chin loftily.

'At any rate, you have not been banished from the ground floor!' she said. 'Why don't you go down and leave me to my singing?'

'Because I prefer exile with you in the schoolroom, sweet Fay!' he answered with a languishing glance, drawing his chair nearer.

With a movement of disgust, Fay pushed back the music stool, crossed the room, and looked out of the window, gazing out above the dark tree shapes where the newborn moon shone a silvery crescent high up in the sky. Philip was intolerable, unbearable, but his thoughts had turned into a different channel.

'The guv'nor had to pay up a good round sum before he could get the Yews,' he said.

Fay turned around, interested.

'Has he bought it?' she asked. 'Oh, I wonder where the money will be found?'

'He means to keep it all to himself if he does get it,' said Philip testily. 'I offered to go and help him dig up the garden, and at once got a flat, and, I may say, rude refusal.'

'And quite right, too!' said Fay. 'If he has spent so much money to get the house, surely it is only natural he should want to find the treasure himself?'

'Yes, but he might give a fellow a chance,' answered Philip in an injured voice. 'The money was left to anyone who found it, and I'll be hanged if I don't have a try!'

Fay looked at him in surprise.

'Why, what do you mean to do?' she asked.

'Ah!' answered Philip enigmatically. 'I won't give myself away, even to you! You wait and see—that's all!'

3

Henry Renton did not recover his normal composure for some time. Alternately irritable and abstracted, he was by no means a pleasant companion.

He had begun his excavations at the Yews and started with the garden, digging there in the early morning and late in the evening when his work was done. The hidden treasure began to take up his thoughts to the exclusion of all else. Even when conducting a case, his mind would wander to Old Pete's money, and, with the map of the garden clear before his eyes, he would ponder as to the most probable place where it would be buried.

There, too, was always that awful fear lest someone else should get into the place while he was away and steal the treasure—perhaps while he was at business or at night when he slept. He took every precaution he could, locking the gates carefully when he left and having the tops of the walls covered with the ends of broken bottles. But even then he did not feel secure, and he grew restless and could not sleep. What should he do if his hopes were disappointed, after all?

Poor Mrs Renton was the one who suffered most from the man's nervous moods, and much did she wish that Old Pete had never died or had, at least, left his money in some sensible manner.

She felt the fact in other ways, too, for, with their decreased mean, she was obliged to draw in expenses. The carriage and horse had to go, and this was a great deprivation at her age. But still, she dared not complain. She knew her husband would never listen to reason now.

She was opening her letters at the breakfast table one morning when she gave a little exclamation of pleasure.

'Here is a letter from Rex!' she said. 'He is home on leave and wants to come and pay us a visit. I am glad. I have not seen him for years, and he used to be such a nice boy!'

'Rex coming here?' echoed her husband. 'Not if I have a voice in the matter! For all that he appears so simple, I expect Charles has his eye on the main chance really, and so sends his son up here in the hopes that he may come across Old Pete's money.'

'Nonsense!' answered Mrs Renton sharply. 'You have gone mad on Old Pete's money and can think of nothing else! You will awake suspicions and put the notion into people's heads the way you are going on at present. What reason are you going to give Rex for not having him here?' Mrs Renton was more courageous in speaking her mind when the family was present to support her.

'Reason?' he answered irritably. 'Why, say we can't afford to have an idle fellow staying here from week's end to week's end. There is plenty of truth in that statement, I should think!'

'But he only asks to come for a fortnight,' objected Mrs Renton. 'And if you won't have him, write the letter yourself. I am not going to refuse him.'

'Oh, let him come,' cried Maud, fretfully putting in her word. She had not seen Captain Renton for a long time, and the idea of having a man staying in the house—even though he was only a cousin—was delightful. 'I don't suppose he even knows about the money.'

'And I will look out for him,' added Philip, laughing. 'If I see any signs of covetousness in his eye, I will let you know at once.'

Henry Renton frowned. He had a dim suspicion that he was making himself ridiculous before his family, and he did not like the idea. He began to see how unreasonable he had been, and that if he had made a fuss about Rex's coming, it would most certainly provoke inquiry in that quarter. He collected his own letters and rose from the breakfast table.

'Have it your own way,' he said grimly. 'As long as Rex doesn't hang about the Yews, I don't care. And if he does come across the money, and so does us out of £80,000, well—you will only have yourselves to blame!'

And, having thus gracefully conceded to the invitation being given, Renton strode out of the room.

Fay was thinking over this conversation as she wended her way through the woods that same afternoon, and she sighed. What havoc, she thought, had the love of money wrought in that household!

All the young leaves were bursting around her, and there was an invigorating feeling about the air. Fay threw out her arms in a sense of freedom. Ah! how glad she was to get out of that house with its oppressive, quarrelsome atmosphere. Primroses strewed the path wherever she stepped. And here and there purple patches of violets peeped out, so that Fay was able to pick a large bunch and put them in her gown where they seemed to repeat the deep colour of her eyes.

She made her way out of the woods until she came to the cliffs beyond. She stood and watched the sea come rolling up while a little fresh breeze loosened the dark tendrils of her hair, and her eyes gazed far out in the distance, where it had grown too misty to discern where the water touched the sky.

After a little while she went further along the cliff, and suddenly a small cottage a little further inland met her eye, which struck her as somewhat familiar.

Where had she heard of that cottage lately? It was some months since she had come so far, and she could not remember. But something attracted her in the small building. It was so entirely by itself, so lonely altogether. Surely no one lived there? And yet—yes, there was smoke arising from the chimney. Fay bent her steps in that direction, half-wondering who could live all alone in this desolate cottage on the cliff? At any rate, there would be no harm in going to see. Visitors must be so rare in this out-of-the-way place, they could not but be welcome.

She went up and knocked rather timidly at the door, and after a few minutes the door was opened by a girl.

'Who lives here?' asked Fay impulsively.

'Mrs Rebecca Grey,' answered the girl.

'Mrs Rebecca Grey?' repeated Fay, perplexed. Where had she heard that name before? 'May I see her?'

The girl looked at her and hesitated, and then, as if making up her mind that it was all right, asked her to come in, and led the way through the small passage.

She pushed open the door, and Fay walked in. There, near the fire, sat an old woman, stretching her hands over the blaze. She looked up, surprised at the entrance of a stranger.

Ah! Fay remembered now. She remembered where she had heard of the cottage. She recognised this old woman at once. Ah, yes! It was Old Pete's housekeeper who lived by herself in this bleak, desolate cottage on the cliff, and who now sat crooning over the fire.

'May I come in?' asked Fay in rather a hesitating tone, for she began to fear her visit might be regarded as an intrusion.

But the old woman pointed to a chair opposite her own by the fire and sat staring at Fay for a few minutes in silence.

'I have seen you somewhere before,' she said suddenly. 'Who are you?'

Fay started. She saw that a change had come over Rebecca since that afternoon at the Yews, that the stunning effect of Old Pete's death had passed away, and the old woman was now in full possession of her senses. Her eyes were keen and penetrating in spite of her withered, wrinkled face and bowed figure, which showed the weight of many years.

'My name is Fay Calderon, and I am governess at Henry Renton's,' answered the girl simply. 'You must have seen me at the Yews. I was present at the reading of the will.'

'Ah!' said the old woman. 'And you helped me along when I might have stumbled—I remember.'

Her eyes left Fay's face, and she gazed now into the red depths of the fire. She appeared to be lost in a reverie.

'Are you not very lonely here?' asked Fay presently. 'The cottage stands quite by itself with no other habitation near. Are you never nervous, living here all alone?'

But the old woman's eyes brightened.

'I love it!' she cried. 'I feel at home when the wind whistles around the house and the sea thunders and roars in the distance. Ah! it is as if I were back in the little fishing village where I was born. The wind and the sea bring my youth back to me. That is why my master gave me this cottage. He knew I should love it so well.'

Again she had fallen into a fit of abstraction, but after a few minutes she looked up again at Fay.

'And why should I be nervous? There is nothing here for anyone to steal,' she asked, looking around the small, well-kept room. 'No one would care to harass me when there would be nothing to gain by so doing. And as for living alone—well, I have not been used to much company all my life!'—a grim smile for a moment played around her much-lined mouth—'My master and I were quite happy together.'

'You must have been very fond of him,' said Fay thoughtfully.

Rebecca gave her a searching glance.

'Does Henry Renton know you have come here today?' she asked sharply.

'Oh, no!' answered the girl. 'I did not know myself when I started. I came to the cottage, I am afraid, out of curiosity'—with a little apologetic smile—'I wanted to see the person who had chosen to live in this solitary abode—alone with herself and the sea.'

'Then Henry Renton does not know?' she said again.

'Mr Renton knows nothing whatsoever about me,' said Fay. 'I only see him at breakfast time, and then his mind is taken up with so many things he could not spare a moment in which to talk to the governess.'

The old woman gave a short laugh of comprehension.

'Ah!' she exclaimed eloquently, and then turned to Fay with a grave face. 'It is much better for you that it is so. And, if I were you, I would not mention a word to him—or, indeed, anybody else— that you have been here. If they want to seek me out'—her voice grew hard—'they know very well where to find me.'

The fire was getting low, and Rebecca shivered. Fay took the poker, and, knocking the red embers together, took a log of wood out of the basket and placed it on the fire. Soon the fresh, pungent scent of the burning wood permeated the room.

Rebecca seemed pleased at her action, for she nodded her old head and smiled. She glanced up at the clock.

'It is teatime,' she said. 'Will you stay and have tea with me? Perhaps'—with hesitation—'you would not mind making it yourself. My limbs are old and rheumatic. I cannot get about as I used to.'

Fay rose with alacrity and soon found the caddy and the tea things. She went into the kitchen and fetched a kettle. Soon it was hissing on the fire, and all the time she chatted so brightly that the old woman's heart warmed as she watched her.

'It is many a day since I had anyone to wait on me,' she said gratefully. 'I am sure the tea will taste all the nicer.'

Fay smiled.

'It is delicious!' she said. 'May I pour you out some more?'

The old woman passed Fay her cup, and together they talked until the afternoon drew in and the lights grew dim in the little room. At last, Fay rose to go.

'It was so good of you to give me tea,' she said with a smile as she held out her hand.

But the old woman drew her face down and kissed her.

'Don't mention my name to Henry Renton,' she said again. 'Do you remember what my master said in the will? And how he asked his cousins to take care of me while I lived?' She gave a little ironical laugh. 'How wonderfully Henry Renton has tried to carry out his wishes! I was hurried out of the Yews at the earliest possible opportunity and scarcely given time even to collect my things. And not content with that'—a red, angry flush stole over her old face—'he insisted on examining my boxes before I came away! Did he think I had the money and was going off with it? I had to look on and allow it, for what could a defenceless woman do? Ah! but it was a deadly insult, and it shall not go unrepaid—no, not if it lies in the power of Rebecca Grey to do so—and suffer for it he shall, either before my death or after!' Her old eyes glittered in a way which greatly surprised Fay Calderon.

'I suppose he has already begun pulling down the Yews and digging up the grounds?' asked Rebecca, turning to her visitor.

'I believe so,' said the girl, 'but I have never been to see. Indeed, no one is allowed inside the gates!'

The old woman gave a comprehensive laugh.

'I expect not,' she said. 'Well, let us hope he will come across the money sometime. He has gone to a good deal of expense about it. He ought to be rewarded!' She again gave that triumphant little chuckle.

'I must go,' said Fay again. 'Only tell me: can I do anything for you? I should like to be of use if you will let me.'

'Come and see me again,' answered the old woman. 'I like you, and you cheer me up. Come and see me again.'

It had grown colder since Fay had been in the cottage. A breeze had sprung up; the sky had grown heavy and threatening. Out in the west was a dull red glare, as if the sun had left the earth in a rage at having his kingdom usurped by clouds.

Fay peered over the cliffs, but it was low tide, and she could see but little of the sea. She hurried home. It was by no means an inviting evening on which to be out.

On her way, she passed the huge iron gates of the Yews and peeped through the bars. The long avenue made the place look very dark and uncanny. Fay started as she saw a movement among the trees. But it was only the solicitor, with an intent look on his face, crossing the path with a spade in his hands. Evidently the threatening look of the weather was of no consequence to him—that is to say, if he noticed it at all.

Fay shuddered as she turned away. It seemed almost pitiful that this man's whole thought and being should be given up to finding this money. And what, after all, if he did not succeed?

It was nearly dark when she reached Brookside Manor, and the girl hurried up the long drive. But all at once she stopped abruptly and turned aside, for she saw the figure of a man coming stealthily from the direction of the house, looking around him as if in fear of detection and walking momentarily nearer to where she stood beneath the shadow of an oak.

Who was this man creeping about Brookside, evidently most anxious that his movements should not be observed?

He came nearer, but before he reached the place where Fay stood, he branched off and went into the shrubberies on the right.

Yes, he had gone out of sight now, but not before Fay had time to recognise him. So it was only Phillip after all. But why were his actions so stealthy? And what was it he had been carrying that was so heavy that he was obliged to wait for a few moments and rest?

Before she could wonder any more, Philip had come out again and stolen up the drive to the house; this time, she noticed, he carried nothing in his hands.

A sudden curiosity assailed Fay; she determined to explore the shrubberies and try to find out the reason for Philip's action.

She had not gone very far, groping through the bushes, when

she stumbled over something in the dark and came to the ground with a jerk.

She rose again quickly, none the worse for her fall beyond a little shaking, and felt along the earth for the obstacle that had thrown her down. Was it only the gnarled root of a tree, or—

But speculation was at an end. Fay had put out her hand and grasped a cold piece of iron that, on further investigation, proved to be a handle of a spade. She felt further and discovered a pickaxe, a rake, and sundry other tools. She knew from the bundle in Philip's hands that he must have placed it here.

She returned to the house more puzzled than ever, determining to question Philip on the subject at the first opportunity.

But for a wonder, he did not come up to the schoolroom that evening, and Fay spent her time quite alone. Not that she did not infinitely prefer solitude to his company, but she was anxious to have her curiosity satisfied.

She looked out of the window before she went to bed. The clouds, which had been threatening for some hours, had now broken, and there was a heavy downpour of rain. Her room was at the corner of the Manor, so the wind whistled around it, and Fay felt there was no use in going to bed—she would not sleep if she did so.

So she took up the second volume of the book she had been reading and was soon absorbed in its contents.

It was an exciting tale, and the volume left off at a critical moment. It was past one o'clock, but Fay felt she must find out the issue of events tonight. The third volume was in the schoolroom; it would not take a minute to get it.

She stole out of the door and along the passage, but when she reached the staircase, a muffled sound struck her ear from below.

Fay held her breath; her cheeks paled. Was it the unmistakable click of the door leading into the garden that she had heard, or was it after all only imagination?

No. A stealthy step was audible, coming with quick, silent tread up the staircase.

Fay's heart stood still, and she was too paralysed with fright to stir or move from the place where the intruder must pass and see her.

Yes, here he was. She could see a man's figure distinctly now. Oh, if she only had the courage to run away! She felt as if she must shriek and betray herself.

But who was it coming towards her? Whose walk was it that she knew so well? A sigh of relief escaped her. It was only Philip, after all —Philip, who had frightened her for the second time today.

But what was he doing at this hour, and what did it all mean? She came forward and blocked the passage.

'Philip,' she exclaimed, in a subdued voice, 'how you frightened me! What have you been doing?'

He started back when he heard his name and looked down angrily at the girl.

'What are you spying on my movements for?' he asked sharply. 'I suppose I can wander about the house when I like as well as you?' He tried to brush past her.

'Why, Philip,' she cried, surprised, as her hand touched his coat. 'You are soaking wet! You must have been in the rain for hours. Where have you been?'

But he roughly pushed her away.

'I left a book in—in the garden,' he stammered, 'and I was afraid it would get spoilt if—if I left it outside. Now get out of my way!'

And Fay went back to her room, wondering. She could not but think from Philip's manner, besides the two mysterious situations in which she had seen him, that he was contemplating something distinctly underhand. The thought of the tools under the trees recurred to her. Had he, too, been at the Yews, digging for the hidden treasure? she wondered. But, if so, how could he get in?

Meanwhile, Philip had turned into his room, swearing under his breath. Was there anything so provoking as that his return should have been seen?

He took off his dripping clothes and paused. What should he do with them? They would provoke inquiry. He bundled them all into a drawer, and, locking it, pocketed the key.

'They will be quite dry enough for me tomorrow night,' he ruminated.

4

'MARY TELLS me that the Yews is supposed to be haunted,' said Mrs
Renton two mornings later, as she dispensed coffee to the assembled
family.

The announcement sent an electric thrill round the breakfast
table, and Mr Renton looked up with a heavy scowl.

'How you can lower yourself, Emily, to listen to the low gossip
of the servants' hall, I can't think! The Yews is no more haunted than
—than the Manor. I should think I ought to know.'

'I only repeat what I heard,' answered his wife with a sigh. 'They
say that it is all over the village that the ghost of Old Pete has been
seen in the avenue the last two nights. No one will go near the place
after dark now.'

Fay shot a quick look across the table at Philip. If, as she
thought, he had been to the Yews the night before last, he must
have seen the apparition. But Philip's eyes were bent on his plate.

'I'm sorry for Old Pete's ghost, that's all I can say,' he muttered
somewhat indistinctly. 'He must have had two very wet nights of it.'
And he pulled out his handkerchief to blow his nose noisily.

'My dear Philip, what a cold you have!' said Mrs Renton with
concern, looking at his watery eyes. 'How ever did you catch it?'

'I don't know!' he answered crossly. 'It's a beastly nuisance, anyhow! I expect it is from coming out into the air after sitting in that stuffy office all day.' And he took out his handkerchief once more.

Fay looked at him curiously. She thought at first that he had been pretending, just to hide his confusion. But she saw now that he really had a bad cold, and that his eyes were streaming. Considering the drenched state in which she had found him the other night, she did not wonder at the result; she could also understand why he did not like it drawn attention to.

'It is bad!' went on Mrs Renton anxiously. 'You ought to stay in the house all day. Henry, Philip's cold is really too bad to go out. You won't want him at the office today, will you?'

'Eh?' answered her husband, starting from a reverie. Since his wife's remark that no one dare go near the Yews after dark, he had been thinking deeply. What an excellent thing it would be to circulate the tale of Old Pete's ghost! It would make him feel so much easier knowing that no one went by there in his absence. It was nonsense, of course—the whole thing was a ridiculous fabrication. But there is always a grain of superstition, even in the most stony-hearted of men, and the idea had occurred to him that if Old Pete 'walked' at all, it would be close to the spot where he had hidden the money.

'Where was this wonderful ghost seen?' he asked, his scathing sarcasm all the sharper because he wanted to know.

'I forget,' said Mrs Renton. 'Somewhere about the middle of the avenue, I believe.'

'And what was it like?'

'Really, you are taking a great interest in the matter, considering you call it all nonsense!' broke in Maud, laughing.

'It is as well to sift these stories well,' answered her father cautiously, with a dull red stealing over his face. 'One can never eradicate them properly from people's minds unless one is up in all particulars. What was it like?'

'Oh, the usual sort of thing! An old, grey-bearded man in white, digging under the trees, and, of course, so transparent that you could see the foliage through him. I wish you would get the idea out of the servants' minds. I often want to send them down to the village after dark, and just because they would have to pass the Yews, I shall never be able to get them to go now. Do speak strongly to them, please!'

'Under the trees?' muttered Mr Renton thoughtfully. He was longing to ask which especial tree Old Pete's ghost had chosen for his excavations, but was afraid of betraying his motive.

Philip burst into a loud laugh.

'The guv'nor thinks the spectre can inform him where the treasure is hidden!' he said. 'I shouldn't wonder'—in an audible whisper—'if he walked round tonight to make its acquaintance.'

Mr Renton scowled darkly. He opened his mouth to make some crushing remark, and then stopped, as if he thought better of it.

'I shall certainly go round and investigate the matter,' he said shortly.

'My dear Henry,' cried his wife, 'you will be tired to death! Leave the Yews to Old Pete's ghost—at any rate tonight. He can do you no harm. It doesn't matter if the spectre finds the treasure or not.'

'You asked me to stop the foolish tale, Emily,' replied her husband sternly, as he rose from the table. 'How can I do so without going there in the dark and showing that I am not afraid myself?'

He went towards the door as he spoke, but his wife stopped him.

'Oh, Henry,' she said again, 'it is not necessary for Philip to go to the office today, is it? He has such a very bad cold.'

The frown grew deeper on Mr Renton's brow.

'Of course he must come,' he said sharply. 'Lazy young beggar! He takes every chance he can of keeping away from his work! Good Heavens! What have I done that I should have a mollycoddle for a son?'

'The guv'nor seems to have got out of bed the wrong side this morning,' said Philip sulkily. 'What a treat I shall have of it all day!'

Captain Renton was to arrive today. Maud and her mother had agreed that it was as well to strike while the iron was hot, so his aunt had written to Rex at once and told him to come as soon as he could. She was so afraid her husband would change his mind again.

Maud was in high spirits. It was such a long time since they had had anyone to stay in the house, and now to have her good-looking cousin, who had distinguished himself so much out in India that he had been awarded the Victoria Cross, the news was too good to be true.

She had not seen Rex for a long time, for he had been abroad for nearly ten years, but she remembered him sufficiently to know the sensation he would create in Brookside and the places round about.

She imagined herself walking down the Axton High Street, always with him in attendance. Axton was the county town, and Maud would make as many shopping excuses as she could to go over there. Perhaps she might meet some of the Roxley party on such occasions, and what an interest they would take in her companion.

The Countess of Roxley had never called on the Rentons, but she knew them to nod to, and once or twice a year they would be asked up to the Castle to a garden party or a large 'At Home'. This would be a great event to Mrs Renton and her daughter; outside the county, they would boast grandly of their invitations. They never added that the whole neighbourhood was present on such occasions, and consequently it was no great compliment their being there too.

❧

CAPTAIN RENTON LEFT his luggage to be sent up and decided to walk to the Manor. He looked about as he went. There was no change in Brookside, he thought, but then his visits to the place had been few and fleeting.

As a boy he had taken such a dislike to his uncle that when invitations came to him from the Manor, he had nearly always refused to go. But that seemed to him such a long time ago that on his return from India he had decided to bury the hatchet and look his relations up. He need only stay a few days, he argued, and it was only right he should go, considering the Henry Rentons were the only connections he had upon his father's side.

Possibly, too, the late events stimulated the captain's curiosity. He would naturally like to see the place where the old hermit lived who had made such a curious will.

'Perhaps,' he had said laughingly to the vicar, 'I may come across the money myself. I expect, really, it is in a very ordinary place, and the less trouble one takes to look for it the more likely it is to be found.'

But the vicar shook his head.

'If I know my brother at all,' he said, 'you will never be admitted inside the gates of the Yews.'

'Ah, well,' Rex answered. 'Considering the amount of money he had to pay to get it, it is only fair he should keep it to himself.'

As he entered the Manor grounds, he saw a slim, graceful figure coming down, and he wrinkled his brows in perplexity as to who it could be.

'It isn't Maud,' he said. 'That girl is not tall enough; as for Ethel —well, I can hardly think Ethel could have grown into anything so charming as this.'

He had drawn nearer by now, and pretty Fay Calderon had all at once raised her eyes and seen him, and he had for a moment gazed down into those wonderful violet depths. He—he must speak. It would be so easy to pretend he had taken her for Ethel. He—

Before he had made up his mind, the girl had rather hurriedly passed him. There had been an expression in his eyes which had called up the lovely colour to her cheeks, and, with her usual quickness, she had discerned his desire to speak.

Who was he, she wondered, this bronzed man with those keen grey eyes, which had looked at her so intently? Of course, how silly of her! She had forgotten Captain Renton was coming today. She need not have minded his scrutiny after all. Most likely he had mistaken her for one of his cousins.

§&

REX WAS RECEIVING a hearty welcome from Mrs Renton and Maud. The latter had attired herself in a smart blue silk blouse in his honour; however, it did not meet with his approval in any way.

Captain Renton had most strict ideas as to women's dress and considered his cousin's present get-up utterly incongruous to an early spring day in the country. Perhaps it was the neat blue serge he had just met in the avenue which made him regard it so unfavourably.

Presently, he mentioned the girl he had seen and asked who she was. Maud bit her lip with vexation.

'Perhaps it was one of the maids,' she suggested.

Rex laughed the idea to scorn. 'It was not one of the maids,' he said.

'Then I expect it was Ethel,' declared Maud decisively and changed the conversation.

But when Ethel appeared, her cousin was disappointed. Ethel had not dark, shadowed violet eyes; hers were a wishy-washy blue! He was diplomatic enough to ask no more, as he saw his previous questions had displeased Maud.

Only, as he went upstairs to bed that night, thinking of the breezy dinner table, where every man's hand had seemed to be against every man, and the long evening to follow, when his sensitive ears had been tortured by Maud's unmusical, expressionless playing, he decided the sooner he could manage to have an important telegram calling him to town, the better.

5

CAPTAIN RENTON WAS UP EARLY the following morning and was wandering about the grounds before any of the family were down.

The Manor was a pretty place, and the fresh air invigorated him a good deal, but still the beauty of the surrounding country was not enough to compensate him for the particularly uncongenial company he had come amongst.

Had they always been like this, he wondered; his uncle surly and silent, Maud unpleasantly garrulous, and Philip uncouth and rude? Perhaps his aunt was the best of the bunch. At any rate, she had tried to smooth matters over and hide the discourtesy of her husband and the gaucherie of her son as well as she was able.

A loud gong sounded in the distance, and Captain Renton sighed as he went in.

He entered the dining room and found the whole family already seated at the table. He had certainly strolled up the avenue somewhat slowly, but then he had not expected such precipitancy as this.

'Good morning!' he said pleasantly. 'I hope I am not very late, but I was out by the shrubberies when the gong rang, and it takes a few minutes to get back.'

'Good morning,' grunted Mr Renton. 'We never wait for anyone here. I will have punctuality in my household, and when I say breakfast is to be at nine—nine it shall be!'

Rex laughed good-humouredly.

'I will remember next time,' he said and crossed the room to where Maud was beckoning him and took the vacant seat by her side.

As he drew his chair to the table, a face on the other side attracted his attention. It was the same one, with the delicate fair skin and dark glowing eyes, which had passed him in the avenue. Who was this lovely girl?

His expression brightened when he saw her. He looked across at his aunt, expecting an introduction, but evidently there was no intention of such a thing. All present went on with breakfast and, as far as Rex could tell, took absolutely no notice of that pretty, slim figure, with the exception of Ethel, who addressed a word to her now and then.

'Who is she?' he whispered to Maud, unconsciously interrupting a long story she was telling him about herself.

'She?' repeated Maud, with pardonable indignation. 'Who?'

'Why, that girl over there. She was the one I told you I met in the avenue yesterday.'

'Really?' she said, with affected indifference. 'Ah, I will tell you about her afterwards! She might hear if I mentioned her name now.'

Inwardly, she was chafing with annoyance. What was there about Fay to provoke inquiry in any man? She did not admire her a bit herself, with that washed-out skin and those hollowed-out eyes.

She passed her hand irritably over her own fair hair and glanced at her face in the mirror opposite with unlimited satisfaction.

Rex was neither glancing at her nor at her reflection. His look was fastened so intently on the wishy-washy skin that the magnetism of his eyes made Fay raise her own hollowed-out orbs, and for a minute she returned his scrutiny with interest.

She did not blush this time, as she had done yesterday. Instead, she threw her little head back rather haughtily, for she considered his glance impertinent, and stared at him coldly until he was obliged to drop his eyes.

As soon as breakfast was over, Miss Renton suggested a stroll with him round the grounds. Fay had disappeared, Rex did not know where, so he accepted the invitation with alacrity. At least he could find out all about her now.

Maud put on a large straw hat, coquettishly turned up at one side, with a big bunch of red poppies on the top. She looked up archly at Rex as she stepped out into the garden. Would he remark on her becoming headgear?

But Rex's eyes were bent on the ground. He seemed to follow her mechanically; his brows met in the middle, and he seemed deep in thought.

'I expect you find the climate cold, after India?' observed Maud, determined to make him turn to her and talk.

'Eh?' he said, staring. 'Cold, did you say? Ah, well, we don't always have tropical heat, you know. It often is not much warmer than this at the hills. About that girl you said you would tell me about?' he continued abruptly. There was no beating about the bush with Captain Renton.

Maud with difficulty concealed her annoyance. A sudden idea occurred to her, and she turned a smiling, amused countenance in his direction.

'Poor Rex!' she said, shaking her head ominously. 'You are stepping into the pit she has dug for you.'

'She? Who?' he answered crossly. He did not care for mysteries in any form, especially when they were connected with himself.

'Why, Fay Calderon, of course—Ethel's governess!'

'Fay Calderon?' he repeated. He liked the sound of the name; it somehow suited the character of those dark eyes. 'Is that the name of the girl at the breakfast table today?'

Maud nodded.

'Yes, that is her name. She is a poor relative of mother, and we took her in out of charity. She is supposed to teach Ethel, by way of helping us a little, but'—with a slighting laugh—'I don't think she has much knowledge to impart.'

6

It was a beautiful afternoon, and Fay thought she would pay another visit to her old friend in the cottage on the cliff. It seemed such a terribly lonely life to the young girl, that now, having permission to call again, she determined to pursue her advantage and cheer up the old woman as much as possible.

A look of pleasure radiated across Rebecca's face when she saw her visitor.

'It is so good of you to come again so soon!' she said heartily.

'Not at all,' answered the girl brightly. 'I am delighted to come.'

'Well, sit down, my dear, and let us have a cosy chat. Tell me what you have been doing since I saw you.'

'Nothing very much,' said Fay. 'Indeed, I never do anything much. My life is pretty much the same day by day. I teach Ethel Renton all the morning, and idle by myself all the afternoon, and that is all.' She looked up at the old woman with a gay little laugh. 'It is a sad confession, but I am afraid there is nothing in the world I love so much as idling.'

'I shouldn't think you would get much of it in Harry Renton's house,' said Rebecca drily. 'Not only he, but all his family are capable of working a willing horse to death. What sort of girl is Ethel?'

'Oh, I don't know,' answered Fay. 'I almost think I like her the best of the family. She is not so depressing as the rest. Do you know'—she said, turning to her suddenly—'that Captain Renton is staying at the Manor now?'

Rebecca shook her head.

'The vicar's son, you mean?' she said. 'What is he like?'

Fay bent her pretty brows in perplexity.

'You see, I only met him at breakfast this morning, so it is very difficult to judge. He is, at any rate, very good-looking.'

'And what is it you don't like about him?' asked the old woman shrewdly.

Fay started.

'I never said I did not like him!' she said, surprised.

'No, your lips didn't, but your eyes did.'

Fay laughed lightly.

'I shall have to be very careful what I say to you,' she said, 'if you are so sharp.' She played with a small gold bangle on her arm thoughtfully.

'I have not even spoken to him yet,' she said, with a laugh without the smallest resentment in it, 'for I am not on sufficient equality with the Henry Rentons to be introduced to their guests. But it was his eyes I did not like. He stared at me in a way which was—well, impertinent!'

Rebecca only smiled.

'If that is his only crime,' she said, 'there cannot be much the matter with him. You could not expect any man, dear, to pass by your pretty face without looking at it.'

Fay coloured at the old woman's compliments and returned her smile.

'It all depends on what sort of way it is done,' she said, still unconvinced, and thinking enough had been said on the matter, changed the conversation. 'Have you heard that the Yews is said to be haunted, and that the figure of an old, grey-bearded man, dressed all in white, makes his appearance in the avenue every night?'

Rebecca looked up with interest.

'No, I have not heard it,' she said. 'And I suppose they say it is my master's ghost?'

Fay nodded her head.

'My master's ghost!' cried the old woman, with scorn. 'What should my master "walk" for? There was nothing on this earth he minded leaving behind him, or that he would ever want to come back to see again.'

'They imagine it is because of the hidden money,' explained Fay.

'Hidden money, indeed!' repeated Rebecca, even more contemptuously. 'Why should he care for money after his death, when he never thought of it during his life? All in white, do you say? Good gracious me! What fools people are! Why in the world should he be all in white off the earth, when he never wore anything but black on it?'

'It is a recognised custom, isn't it,' said Fay, smiling, 'that ghosts should be attired in nothing but white?'

'Ah!' said Rebecca knowingly. 'You may be very certain that my master's ghost is a very substantial one. Someone has a motive in scaring people away from the place.'

Fay looked up quickly.

'You mean that Mr Renton—?' she began.

But the old woman broke in abruptly.

'I don't mean anything,' she said. 'I only think.'

REX HAD MADE his way up to Roxley Castle, and had been accorded a most flattering reception. The Countess had taken a great liking to Captain Renton when she had met him out in India, and she was glad to see a visitor at Roxley, for life was dull to her pleasure-loving nature. She would never have come at all had it not been that her husband insisted on spending most of the winter there, and being a man of iron will and much older than herself, he generally got his own way, in spite of his wife's remonstrances.

'The people in the neighbourhood are so dreadfully dull and respectable!' she had protested. 'If I go to Roxley, I know I shall shock them. It is my longing to do so whenever I am amongst them!'

Now she received Rex with undisguised delight, and the two sat talking for some time about the old days in India.

'You will take pity on me and come again soon, won't you?' she said insinuatingly. 'Roxley will be so sorry to have missed you! He has gone down to look at some newly purchased cows. Nothing he loves better than pottering about his old farm. It is a great pity I don't have rustic tastes, too!'

Rex smiled.

'But you will be going up to town soon?' he asked.

She made a little grimace.

'Roxley declares he won't leave the castle until the end of May. It is dreadful, isn't it? He has tried to pacify me by letting me give a dance next month. You will be in the neighbourhood then, won't you? You will come?'

'Well, I am afraid I shall have gone—' he began. Fancy living four weeks in the same house as his uncle!

'Oh, but that is nonsense!' she broke in at once. 'You must not be allowed to go. You are staying at the Manor, I think you said?' She looked at him furtively. Perhaps she understood his reasons for making such a short visit and sympathised accordingly. 'Ah, well, when your time is up there, come and stay at the castle. You can then help me with all the arrangements for the ball. Will you?'

He could not well refuse the invitation, while her brown eyes looked at him so. Neither did he want to, though he scarcely knew what his aunt and cousins would say.

'I shall be only too delighted,' he answered.

'Then tell your people about the dance,' she said graciously. 'The invitations will be out next week. In the meantime, come to lunch one day—Tuesday, shall we say?'

He accepted, conditionally that it did not interfere with his aunt's arrangements, and took his leave.

'I suppose I ought to have asked his cousins to lunch, too,' she said to herself dubiously when she was once more alone. 'But I couldn't—I really couldn't. How is it that such a man as Captain Renton can be related to such dreadful people? Ah, well, they must be satisfied with the dance. They will be lost in a crowd then, fortunately!'

Rex walked down through the broad sweep of Roxley Park and decided to go home by the path along the cliff. As he came along he started, for there in front of him stood a girl's figure silhouetted against the crimson rays of the setting sun.

Something in the slight, graceful figure seemed familiar to him, and he hastened his steps and drew nearer. All his good resolutions seemed to be slipping away. Only half an hour before, he had quite made up his mind to persistently avoid this girl, who had so confidently boasted that she could subdue him.

She stood at the edge of the cliff, her eyes fixed on the sea, and quite absorbed in her own thoughts. She did not notice Rex until he was quite close, and his appearance made her start. She looked at him wonderingly with her great, dark eyes, which seemed to have caught the reflection of the sunset.

'I am sorry I startled you, Miss Calderon,' he said apologetically. 'Do you often take twilight walks on the cliffs?'

The dreamy look his advent had interrupted came back to her eyes.

'The sea has a fascination for me,' she said. 'I love to watch it. It is so restless—so impatient to control. It always seems to be as if some powerful hand were holding it back and forcing it to obedience against its will. One day,' she went on pensively, 'I think the hand will relax its hold, and the waves will then break loose in all their fury and overwhelm us!'

'What? Do you prophesy another flood?' Was this the girl who had been described to him as heartless? This girl, with the far-away eyes and the sweetest voice he had ever heard? He felt his feelings of aversion slipping from him one by one, and he pulled himself up sharply.

'After all,' said reason in his ear, 'it is all done for effect. She is clever and knows how to suit her conversation to her company.'

She turned round at his words, as if to see if he was serious or not, but as she glanced at him the dreamy look fled from her eyes and a mischievous sparkle took its place.

'What have you been doing with yourself?' she asked, breaking out into a little ripple of laughter. 'You look as if you had been out in a heavy snowstorm. You have no idea what an amusing spectacle you present.'

The sudden transformation bewildered him, and as he glanced down at himself for an explanation of her words, he was trying to make up his mind in which mood she looked prettier—whether he liked her best with the far-away look or as she was now, with the laughter on her lips and lurking in her eyes?

He found that he was covered with petals of double cherry blossoms. He remembered now how they came to be there.

'I knocked against a tree coming out of Roxley Park,' he said, smiling, 'and was at once greeted with a shower of blossoms. It did not strike me at the time that the petals would cling so tenaciously to my coat.'

He tried to brush the blossoms off his sleeve, but she stopped him.

'You will never get rid of them like that,' she said. 'They stick so to the rough tweed. They ought to be picked off one by one. Stand still a minute, and I will do it.'

In a moment she had slipped off her gauntlet glove, and,

standing as near to him as possible, her slim, white fingers soon cleared the petals from his shoulders.

Captain Renton stood wondering both at her and himself. Her quick action had astonished him. She had done it with such an absolute lack of self-consciousness; he could not be persuaded that it was only the manoeuvre of a finished coquette, try as he might to convince himself of the fact.

The touch of her small fingers sent an odd thrill through him. Her charming head was so close—so dangerously close.

He threw discretion to the winds. After all, if it pleased her to attempt his conquest, let her. He was over thirty, and if he were not able to take care of himself by this time, he ought to be! Anyhow, the process of his subjugation was pleasant.

'What? Are they all gone?' he asked, almost with disappointment, as she stood back and drew on her glove again. 'I expect there are some in the brim of my hat. See if there are not.'

'I dare say,' she said, laughing. 'Take it off and shake it!'

This was not quite what he had intended; still, he did as he was told.

The sun had disappeared beyond the horizon, but it had left a trail behind which reflected on the sea and dyed the waves a golden and a crimson hue.

'Are you going home now?' asked Rex. 'If so, we might as well go together.'

Fay turned to go with him at once, and together they traversed the little wood, passing the great iron gates of the Yews, at which they paused for a moment and peered furtively in. But there was nothing to be seen, only the great black trees looking more sombre and gloomy than ever.

'It is a fit residence for a ghost, at any rate!' remarked Captain Renton as they went on.

'Yes,' said Fay. 'But do you think even £80,000 is worth all the trouble and worry Mr Renton is taking to find it?' She was thinking of the idea that Rebecca had put in her mind.

'No,' answered Rex absently. He was wishing it were not quite so dark, so that he could get a clearer view of his companion's face.

The dinner gong was sounding loudly—aggressively—as they walked up the drive to the Manor.

7

'WE SHALL BE LATE!' exclaimed Captain Renton, laughing. 'How long does it take you to dress?'

'I?' answered Fay. 'Ah, you see, I am independent; it does not matter about me. I have my dinner upstairs, and so can have it when I like. Don't you wish that you could, too?'

'A good idea! I declare I will!'

But she only laughingly shook her head and ran upstairs.

Rex was not long dressing, but fish was just being taken away when he entered the dining room. He apologised profusely—he was very sorry for his rudeness—but he obtained no response from the head of the table: Mr Renton went on eating, his face dark with scowls, while his wife's countenance wore a weary, troubled look.

Rex shrugged his shoulders, sat down between Maud and his aunt, and began to tell the former about his visits.

Instantly, every face present assumed a different aspect. It was certainly most outrageous to be so late, but if he had been detained at the castle—well, that was quite a different matter. For some reason or another, Captain Renton did not find it necessary to mention the meeting on the cliff, nor the walk home afterwards.

'A dance?' cried Maud. 'A dance at the castle? Ah, but I am afraid they won't ask us!'

'On the contrary,' said Rex, 'Lady Roxley sent a special messenger to you and said the invitations would be out next week.'

The news was received with a shriek; even Mr Renton's face relaxed, and he asked his nephew if he would take any more lamb in a most genial voice. Rex was quite forgiven.

He decided, too, on his way to bed that the pressing telegram summoning him to town might wait a few days longer.

THOUGH HENRY RENTON did not believe in Old Pete's ghost, he thought it better to investigate the matter and find what had given rise to the tale, and to do this it would be necessary to spend a night at the Yews.

He did not say anything to anybody, but at ten o'clock that night he slipped out. A half-moon was holding her sway in the heavens, and the sky was as cloudless as it had been a few hours before, when the sun had dipped down behind the sea, reflecting crimson lights on the faces of Rex and Fay as they stood together on the cliff.

It was not a very pleasant evening on which to visit the deserted house, for deceptive shadows lurked by the wayside, and Mr Renton gave many a furtive look as he went along.

The avenue of yews looked even darker and gloomier in the moonlight as the solicitor closed the iron gates behind him and turned the key in the lock.

He proceeded to walk towards the house, when something made him stop abruptly, and his heart stood still.

What was this thing wending its way in and out through the trees, its long, white draperies catching the moonlight here and there—gliding, so it seemed to him, with a sick foreboding, straight in his direction!

In that moment of terror, a thousand thoughts assailed him.

If he could only get away—away from the avenue and out of the gates before it—this horrible thing—approached him! But his feet remained glued to the spot, and his breath came in short, quick gasps. It was coming nearer—it would touch him directly. He could see the black, hollow eyes, set with Death's grim smile, and—good Heavens!—the eyes were turned on him, and—and—

There was a buzzing in his ears, and a sudden dizziness came over him. The spectre seemed to dance up and down before his terror-glazed eyes, and the ghastly smile seemed to widen—widen on that deathlike countenance. Renton staggered, caught at a tree for support, but missing it, fell, a senseless mass in the middle of the avenue.

How LONG HE remained there he did not know. With a shuddering sigh, he came to life and looked around him. It was dark now, for the moon had sunk low, and her ebbing radiance was lost behind a cloud. His eyes, dazed, looked fearfully round, but all was gloomy and silent. That ghastly spectacle had disappeared.

With an effort, he pulled himself up and tottered down the avenue to the gates. Here, he had to rest a minute or two for support, but it was only for a moment. A feverish desire came over him to reach home, so that his absence should not be noticed.

And, fortunately for him, no questions were asked. For often he would sit up late in his study reading, and Mrs Renton would have no idea when he came to bed.

But she did wonder a little at his ready acquiescence to stay at home the following day. His haggard, drawn appearance made her suggest it, and he assented at once. His nerves had been greatly upset, and he felt he needed a little rest.

This decision made his wife even more alarmed.

'I am afraid you are ill,' she said anxiously.

But he shook off her hands from his arm impatiently.

'I'm all right!' he snapped. 'I have a headache—that's all! Women always think one's dying at the least thing!'

'He is pale,' remarked Rex as his uncle closed the door behind him.

'Looks as if he had seen a ghost!' cried Philip, with his loud, slighting laugh, as he rose and pushed his chair from the table.

8

'It seems so very rude going out and leaving you alone like this, Rex. I do hope you understand that we would not do it if we could possibly help it.'

Mrs Renton was arranging a square of black Chantilly lace gingerly about her head in front of the long glass in the hall. Consequently, her words fell from her lips at short, irregular intervals. She was attired in a ruby velvet gown, and an elaborate spray of diamonds caught together the lace on her bodice.

'Of course, Aunt Emily, I understand,' answered Rex, stepping forward to help her with her cloak. 'I shall be quite happy at home. Please don't worry about me.'

'If it were anything but a dinner party,' went on Mrs Renton, glancing sideways at her reflection with a dissatisfied air—if only her cheeks would get rid of that provoking notion and not think it etiquette to match the tone of her gown!—'then we could either stay at home or take you with us. But with a dinner party, you see, one cannot disappoint at the last minute, and, of course, one extra would upset the whole table. Rex, dear, would you mind buttoning up my glove? No, don't attempt the first one—that would never meet. I wish Maud and your uncle would be quick; I know we shall be late!'

The dinner was at Sir John Seymour's, the member for Roxley. He was an able man and knew well how to keep his constituents in good humour with himself. So Lady Seymour gave a certain number of dinner parties every year, and the one to which the Rentons were invited always caused intense excitement and satisfaction at Brookside Manor.

As Rex saw them off, he felt an inward satisfaction that he was not included in the party. An evening at home by himself was much more to his taste, and perhaps—who knows?—he might come across—ah, well, perhaps he wouldn't have it to himself after all.

'Goodbye, Rex!' said Maud, putting up her face to be kissed with an affected, childlike air. She had done this more than once in the last few days, and Captain Renton thought it time to put a stop to the habit.

He would not have objected to the cousinly salute so much, but it was not pleasant to have to wipe the powder off his lips directly after.

'Look at your gown, Maud!' he said quickly. 'It is trailing in the mud.'

The intelligence was sufficient to distract her from the hope of a kiss from her bronze-faced cousin.

'Goodbye, Rex!' his aunt called after him as they drove off. 'Make Philip see after you!'

Her words came as a sort of damper to Captain Renton. Philip? He had forgotten Philip. Good gracious! Was he to spend the evening alone with that clodhopper?

With the exception of a glimpse every morning at the breakfast table, Rex had seen nothing of Fay Calderon since their walk home together nearly a week ago, and probably because the difficulties of another tete-a-tete with her were so great, he determined to manage one sooner or later.

He had long ceased to question Maud about her, for he found

firstly that such conversations would be certain to leave his cousin in a very bad humour, and secondly, he was afraid by showing too much interest in Miss Calderon to subject himself to the inevitable 'I told you so.'

Not that he was the least bit in love with her; he told himself so fifty times a day. How could he be, considering he had seen little of her? He put down the persistent tendency of his thoughts to turn in her direction simply to the fact that Maud's description of her had whetted his curiosity, and—well, certainly he was willing to admit there was some indefinable charm about the girl herself. But as to being in love...

Nevertheless, on hearing that the family was dining out tonight, he had mentally planned out his evening accordingly. He intended to explore the Manor; no doubt he would come across the schoolroom in time.

But Philip! The idea of Philip dashed his hopes to the ground. How could he get rid of Philip? It was so tiresome; everything else had fitted in so well. Even Ethel had caught a convenient cold and was spending the day in bed.

And if Captain Renton was annoyed at Philip, the latter was a good deal more incensed at the presence of Rex.

'Why should he invite himself and come to the Manor just when he liked?' he thought irritably. 'A fine evening—such a splendid chance, too, with the guv'nor well out of the way—and everything spoilt because I have to stay at home and entertain this confounded fellow! I wonder—I wonder if I can manage to give him the slip and get out?'

The two sat down to dinner, neither in a very happy state of mind. Perhaps, to conceal his real feelings, Rex was more than necessarily polite, and Philip—probably for the same reason—responded with the best grace he could.

But in the smoking room afterwards, Captain Renton began to yawn. The precious time was going; if he hesitated much longer, he would find the schoolroom empty and Fay gone to bed. He meditated suggesting a stroll outside. Surely Philip would not want to come, too?

Philip was also cursing the delay. He was wondering if Rex would suspect anything if he pleaded a business engagement. They would be home from the Seymours' in two hours, and then it would be a whole evening wasted.

Suddenly, from the distance came the sound of a few chords on the piano, then the soft notes of a sweet voice singing wafted in through the open window.

Rex held his breath, and a strange thrill ran through his heart.

'Whose voice is that?' he asked quickly—almost nervously. 'Is it an inmate of the Manor who has a voice like that?'

Philip's loud laugh rang harshly on his ears.

'It is only Fay!' he said. 'What? You have never heard her sing before?'

A delightful way out of the difficulties occurred to Philip, and his spirits rose accordingly. Why had he not thought of it before?

'Come up to the schoolroom and hear her!' he said cordially, linking his arm in his cousin's. 'Her voice is something wonderful! That is why she is not allowed downstairs in the evening—she attracted too much attention to herself. D'ye see?'

But Rex was scarcely listening, and he went with Philip almost mechanically. He was musical to his fingertips; the sound of Fay's voice had seemed to penetrate his soul and still lingered in his ears.

Philip burst open the schoolroom door noisily.

'Captain Renton wants to hear you sing, Fay,' he said abruptly, then shut the door and left them together.

Fay had risen from the piano and was standing by the open window when he entered. There were no lights in the room; only the moonbeams poured in, lighting up the girl's face and giving her an almost ethereal appearance as she turned round to greet Captain Renton.

He stood beside her at the window looking out on the gardens, which were transformed into fairy realms by the moonlight, and somehow he felt as if he stood on enchanted ground.

'It is a long while since I saw you,' he said, looking down at her dark head, evidently making up for lost time now.

'Only twelve hours,' she said with a light little laugh.

Fay was essentially practical. She knew nothing about falling in love or any of the symptoms which lead up to the fever, and waved aside all compliments as totally unmeaning. She had changed her opinion and now decided that she liked Captain Renton; her eyes shone with pleasure when he was ushered in.

He gazed down into her dark eyes—darker still in the moonlight—and wondered: could she really be so unconscious, or was it only affected? A faint, half-formed wish rose in his heart that it was the latter. He felt he would like to see blood rush to her face at the sight of him; he would like to see her start at the sound of his voice; he would like to see those eyes, which were looking up straight and clearly into his, fall at his glance, and the long lashes quiver on her cheeks.

'I mean that it is a long time since I talked to you,' he answered slowly.

'Well,' she said smiling, settling herself in a chair and motioning him to do the same. 'We will have a talk now. I will sing to you later. You never told me the other day that there was to be a dance at the castle.'

'We had so many other things to say,' he replied, drawing his chair close to hers. 'Are you glad about it? Do you like dancing?'

'I?' She looked at him, surprised. 'Yes, I love dancing, but—well, the castle dance won't make much difference to me, because, of course, I shall not go.'

'Not go?' he repeated disappointedly. 'But why?'

'Well, for one thing, Mrs Renton would not let me go if I were asked, and I am certainly not likely to receive an invitation, for Lady Roxley has not seen me for years and has no idea that I am living anywhere near here.'

'But she must be told,' answered Rex, with a reassuring smile. 'How long is it since you met her?'

'Oh, I was only a child! She used to be a great friend of my mother's and came with us to Blankshire for the hunting, both before and after her marriage.'

'Are you fond of hunting?' asked Rex, watching her as the different expressions flitted across her face.

'Oh, I love it!' Her eyes sparkled. 'But it is nearly a year since I was on a horse. A year is a long time, isn't it?'

'And have you been here since then?'

'Oh, no, I came here in the autumn after my father died.' There was a sorrowful cadence in her voice. 'He lost all his money, you see, and the shock killed him, and so—and so I came here.'

She turned away her head, but he could see the big tear trembling in her eye, and his heart bled for her.

'It must have been a great change coming here,' he said gently after a minute or two.

'It was very good of your aunt to ask me,' she said gratefully. 'I should have been obliged to go among strangers otherwise.'

'Where you would have been very much better treated,' thought Rex to himself grimly. But all he said was: 'I am going to lunch at the castle tomorrow and shall see that you receive an invitation. You will promise me to go, won't you?'

He was rewarded by the sudden gladness in her face. She clapped her hands joyfully.

'Oh, how good you are!' she cried. 'How I shall enjoy it!'

'And now,' he said, laughing, 'you must give me my reward. You promised to sing to me, you know.'

She rose at once and went to the piano, and he sat entranced as she sang song after song to him. She was such a child—how could she feel the passion that was heard in her voice? The moonbeams reached to the piano and covered Fay with their pale glory. Captain Renton was fairly bewitched. His soul seemed to be lifted out of himself, and his breath came shortly and quickly. He could not remove his eyes from the lovely face in front of him.

'Unless you can think when the song is done
No other is sweet in the rhythm;
Unless you can feel, when left by one,
That all men else go with him;
Unless you can feel, when uprais'd by his breath,
That your beauty itself wants proving;
Unless you can swear for life, for death,
Oh, fear to call it loving!
Unless you can muse in a crowd all day
On the absent face which fixed you;
Unless you can love as the angels may,
With the breath of heav'n betwixt you;
Unless you can dream that his faith is fast,
Thro' behoving and unbehoving;
Unless you can die when the dream is past,
Oh, never call it loving.'

The chords died away, and Fay rose and went over the window where Rex stood.

'Miss Calderon, have you ever been in love?' Captain Renton's face was pale, and he was strangely moved.

'Never,' she answered dreamily.

'How, then, can you sing songs like that, and in such a way?'

But she did not reply. Instead, she leant out of the casement and pointed to the view.

'When the pale moon drowns the world in a flood of silver light,' she quoted softly.

He followed the movement of her fingers and looked out too.

9

THE WINDOW WAS SMALL, and the two heads were very close. The magic of her music still lingered in the air, seeming to echo through the silence of the night, and the whole world seemed to Rex to be, for the moment, enchanted.

A wisp of Fay's hair blew out and brushed across his face, setting his pulses beating madly at the mere touch. His lips were so near. She turned her dark eyes on him, bathed in moonlight, and—and almost before he knew of his intention, he had kissed those sweet lips so dangerously, so temptingly close to his own.

Fay, in her surprise, had not even resisted. She drew back from the window and looked at him for a moment with a sort of startled wonder. Then the bright colour rushed to her face and just as quickly ebbed away. What had happened? Had Rex's wish of an hour ago come true? For those sweet, fearless eyes fell before his glance, and her slight form trembled ever so little. Had he broken down the wall of her childlike unconsciousness?

'Fay,' he whispered, bending his fair head towards her, 'Fay!'

But, without a word, without a sound, she had gone—flown from him—and Rex realised, with a sigh, that he was alone in the room.

❧

'MAMA! MAMA! HERE ARE THE INVITATIONS!' cried Maud excitedly, rushing into the drawing room, where Mrs Renton and Rex were having their tea. 'Do open them quickly!'

Mrs Renton hastened to put on her glasses and carefully inspected her cards.

'They have sent me two by mistake,' she said, taking up another envelope. 'Oh, no, it is for—what a very extraordinary thing!—it is for Fay! Lady Roxley can't possibly have asked her too!'

'Fay?' cried Maud angrily. 'Oh, you must be mistaken! It is no great compliment to go when people like that are asked!'

Rex looked at her in indignant surprise.

'What do you mean?' he said sharply.

'Why, fancy asking a governess! I call it a positive insult! Well, one thing, of course, you won't allow her to go, mama!'

'My dear, I can't think how Lady Roxley even knows of her existence!' said Mrs Renton helplessly.

'That, I expect, was my doing,' said Rex, coming forward. He was actually pale with anger. 'I happened to mention her name as staying here, and Lady Roxley was delighted to hear it. Miss Calderon's mother was her greatest friend, and she is very anxious to renew acquaintance with her daughter.'

His words fell as a bombshell on the other two. Maud curled her lip scornfully.

'Greatest friend, indeed! I expect Mrs Calderon was only Lady Roxley's maid!'

'My dear Maud,' said her mother crossly, 'how can you say so? I have always told you the Calderons were very well connected. They were connections of mine'—turning to Rex—'and that is why I had Fay here when Colonel Calderon died. Such a sad affair, you know!'

She was rather pleased than otherwise at the turn of events. She thought it reflected credit on herself and felt, in consequence, as if she were as good as related to the Countess of Roxley. At any rate, she might get to know her better through Fay.

Maud, however, was not. She was furiously angry at the news. It was not only the fact of Fay's invitation, but that she should have obtained it through the instrumentality of Rex.

'Of course you won't let her go, Mama!' she said decisively. 'Better not let her hear of the invitation at all. It would save a fuss!'

'My dear,' answered her mother curtly, 'as Lady Roxley has been good enough to ask her, I could not think of being so rude as to leave her behind. Would you mind ringing the bell, Rex? I will send up for Fay at once—that is to say, if she is at home.'

Fay was at home, as Rex knew very well, for he had been watching the garden door all the afternoon, so that she should not escape him.

He wanted to talk to her—to ask pardon for his impulsive act three nights ago—but somehow she would never give him a chance.

At breakfast, she would sit with averted eyes, never glancing once in his direction and only once, by chance, had she met his look. Though it was only momentary, he had rejoiced to see the sudden crimson which dyed her cheeks. At least, she could not look at him now in the calm, unmoved way she had done before that evening in the schoolroom.

He stood with his back to the window and watched the door impatiently until she came. Fay gave a furtive glance in the direction where the tall form shut out the light.

'You want me, Mrs Renton?' she said brightly, coming forward.

'Yes, my dear, sit down. I have a pleasant little piece of news for you. See what I have here.'

She put the invitation in Fay's hand.

A brilliant colour leapt to the girl's cheeks, but she would not look up, for, to her dismay, Mrs Renton had motioned her to a chair just opposite where Rex stood, and the full light of the afternoon sun fell on her face. She knew he was watching her, and she resented it.

Yet it was to him she owed this invitation, and she could not keep back her pleasure in receiving it.

'Oh-h!' she cried, and her eyes sparkled. 'Has Lady Roxley really asked me, and will you let me go, Mrs Renton?'

'Naturally. It would never do to refuse, considering how she has gone out of her way to include you,' said Mrs Renton grandly. 'The only trouble is about your gown. Of course, you have nothing which will do. We shall have to manage to patch something together.'

'Oh, but I have!' cried Fay. 'I have the gown that I wore at the county ball in Blankshire the winter before last—the evening I came out.'

She had forgotten Rex for the moment and was gazing through the window out at the blue distance. What memories had her words called up, Rex wondered, to bring such a sorrowful look into those sweet, violet eyes? Was it—could it be—some one partner at that ball? The sudden sharp pang of jealousy that ran through his heart at the thought absolutely startled him.

'Oh, well,' his aunt was saying with a sigh of relief, 'I don't suppose that will need much alteration—fashions have not changed much since then.'

'I can't think why the whole household is not asked!' broke in Maud spitefully. 'Nor what Mary and the cook have done that they should not be invited too!'

'Maud,' said Captain Renton in a dangerously quiet tone of voice, 'you are forgetting yourself as a lady.'

She shrank back from the angry glitter in his eyes.

But Fay laughed lightly.

'Does Maud not like it because I am asked?' she said pityingly. 'Poor Maud!'

But as she spoke she shot a shy, grateful glance at Rex for his championship, which made his heart beat quickly. It was the first time she had looked at him voluntarily since he had stolen that kiss in the moonlight three evenings ago.

'Well, my dear, that is all I wanted to tell you. You can go if you like. I suppose you are panting to get out in the open air, as usual?'

Mrs Renton was unusually genial this afternoon, and Fay wondered, as she put on her hat, what the reason could be. She did not know that Rex had let out the intimacy which had existed between Lady Roxley and her mother. Mrs Renton intended to trade briskly on this information.

Fay did not go to her usual haunt, the wood; instead, she turned the other way and took the path which led into the orchard.

If she expected to avoid Rex by doing so, she was mistaken, for he did not move from the window until he saw her come out and noticed what direction she took.

He found her all among the blossoms. The pear and cherry trees were fully cut, and so many petals had fallen on the ground that it looked as if it had been snowing. The apple trees so far only showed pink-tipped buds, and Fay was inspecting one of these when Rex found her. She turned away, scarcely knowing how to treat him. Still, he had procured the invitation to the ball; she must say something.

'It was very good of you to ask Lady Roxley to invite me,' she began nervously. 'It is all through you that—that I am going, and I —I am very grateful.'

'I only mentioned your name,' he answered, waving aside her thanks. 'The memory of your mother did the rest. Lady Roxley is only too delighted to have the opportunity of knowing you.'

She did not answer but began rather ruthlessly picking the blossoms of the apple tree in her nervousness. Why wouldn't she look at him? He determined to make her raise her eyes to his.

'Miss Calderon,' he said humbly, 'I have followed you out here to apologise. I was mad the other night—utterly mad—and scarcely knew what I was doing. Your voice—your music—had got into my head. Fay'—his tone was almost tender—'don't banish me forever because of what I did on the impulse of the moment.'

She covered her face with her hands, blushing furiously.

'Oh,' she cried incoherently, 'how could you do it—how could you do it?'

He was tempted to take her hands away and try to comfort her, but, with a masterful effort, he resisted the impulse.

'Let us forget all about it,' he said, with marvellous tact. 'We will treat the episode as if it never happened. Will you agree to that, Miss Calderon? Don't be unkind and refuse. You don't know how miserable I have been ever since.' He held out his hands entreatingly. 'Do be friends with me again!'

She put her little hand in his with a feeling of relief. She did not want to quarrel with him.

Ah! Fay, it will never be again as it was before! There were no shy glances in those days, and your colour did not come and go in that quick, inconsistent way it has taken to doing the last few days.

THE WEEKS SPED ON, and the intimacy between Fay and Captain Renton increased and strengthened every day. Recently, he had left the Manor and was staying at the castle. This arrangement he found infinitely preferable, for he found it so much easier to meet Fay in some of her favourite haunts now he was away from Maud's suspicious eye.

But Miss Renton saw much more than he thought, and her animosity against Fay grew stronger and stronger; she longed to revenge herself on the girl for enticing Rex away from her.

It was the day before the ball. Captain Renton and Fay had been walking together through the wood, and they stood lingering over their farewell by the little gate which led into the manor grounds.

Maud, who had suspected something, was standing in the shrubberies, hidden from view by a tall bay tree, watching with eager eyes and listening with pricked-up ears.

She saw the look in Rex's eyes as he took Fay's small hand in his, and when he spoke she could detect the repressed passion in his voice.

'I shall not see you again until the ball,' he was saying in a quick, eager manner. 'You will not give any dances away until I have seen you, will you?'

Fay looked surprised.

'Not give away dances?' she repeated. 'But perhaps I shall not come across you till half the evening is over. Do you want me to sit out all that time?'

Rex laughed lightly.

'I don't think you will have to wait for me so long as that. Besides,' he went on, more seriously, 'I claim your dances as a right; they are mine. If it had not been for me, you would not have been present at the ball—you said so yourself. Don't you think'—looking down at her in a way that made Maud clench her teeth—'don't you think your time at the castle really belongs to me?'

Fay turned away from his glance, which had called the colour to her face, and looked back at the wood from where they had just come.

'You will be almost like one of the hosts,' she said with a little sigh. 'I do not expect you will have much time to spare for me.'

He threw his head back and laughed again.

'Shall I not?' he said. 'Well, then'—in a rapid whisper, only just audible to Maud where she stood—'will you promise to give me as many dances as I want?'

'Ye-es,' answered the girl restlessly, turning away. 'I don't know any of the people here, so'—with a smile of self-depreciation—'I do not think you will find much competition.'

Maud watched Captain Renton's head as it bent closer to the girl.

'But promise me,' he said. 'I want to hear you promise.'

'I promise,' answered Fay, half-frightened at his vehemence.

Opening the gate, she waved her hand to him lightly and vanished up the drive.

Passionate anger had been rising in Maud's breast. Something must be done at once; there was no time to be lost. She decided to use her utmost endeavour to upset the arrangement that had just been made and make Fay break her promise at the ball.

10

IT WAS NOT a cheerful party which drove from the Manor to
Roxley Castle on the night of the ball. Mr Renton sat silent and
surly in the corner of the hired fly, and, by his manner alone, was
sufficient to dampen the highest spirits.

He was growing disheartened. Every portion of the garden had
been dug up, and yet nothing—absolutely nothing—had been
found to reward his efforts. Now he had started on the house itself.
Methodically and systematically, he began in the garrets and
pursued his search down to the cellars. Was it likely, in the face of
such a 'fixed idea', that a frivolous matter like a dance should affect
him in any way? If it had been anywhere else but at Roxley Castle,
the solicitor would have scouted the very idea of attending such a
function. But there was no greater tuft-hunter living than Henry
Renton; he felt proud and honoured to think he should be present
at a festival which he had made a point of discovering that none of
his ordinary friends and associates in Brookside were invited.

'Mrs Bolton called today,' said Mrs Renton in a muffled voice,
for, in spite of the warm night, her mouth was wrapped around in a
woollen cloud.

'Mrs Who?' shouted her husband. 'For Heaven's sake, speak up,

Emily! One can't hear oneself talk in this infernal jolting vehicle, much less anyone smothered up in shawls, as you are!'

Mrs Renton obediently pulled aside the cloud.

'Mrs Bolton,' she repeated. 'She was in a fury when she heard we were going tonight. She tried to make out she had been asked, and refused. Ha, ha! Just as if I did not know!'

Mr Renton grunted.

'The way you women get your knife into each other!' he said sardonically. He did not think it necessary to add that he had met Mr Bolton that afternoon and sent him away, gnashing his teeth, with the very same news which had routed his wife.

Meanwhile, under the cover of her parents' conversation, Maud turned to Fay and startled her out of a happy daydream.

'I had a letter from Captain Renton tonight,' she said, 'just before we started. He sent you a message.'

'Sent me a message?' echoed Fay, with rich colour flowing to her cheeks.

'Yes. There seems to have been some arrangement between you about dances tonight—is that so?'

'Well,' answered Fay, without committing herself. 'What does he say?'

'He asks me to tell you that he will not be able to keep the arrangement—that he will, in fact, be too busy to dance with you tonight. He hopes,' added Maud with relish, for she was enjoying the effect of her words, 'he hopes you won't mind.'

Fay laughed. It was a masterpiece of a laugh, for it sounded almost natural, and Maud was not quick enough to notice the hard ring in it.

'It is a dreadful calamity!' said the girl gaily. 'I shall have to try and exist without a dance with Captain Renton tonight.'

Maud frowned. Her words somehow seemed to have missed their mark. At any rate, she thought to herself comfortingly, Fay will know no one there, so if Rex does not dance with her, she won't dance at all.

And Fay, as she leant back and gazed through the window out into the night, felt that all her happy anticipations had crumbled into dust, and the forthcoming evening held no pleasure for her. He might—yes, he might—have written to her to tell her so; it was the least he could have done. But to send her a communication through Maud!

The castle was a pretty sight, with its thousand lights and floral decorations. There was such a festive feeling about the air that even Fay's drooping spirits revived, and a brighter colour was burning in her cheeks as Mr and Mrs Renton and Maud entered the ballroom where Lady Roxley was standing receiving, looking beautiful in gold brocade, her diamonds flashing out different coloured fires as she moved.

'And this is Fay?' she cried in a voice of genuine pleasure, having shaken hands with the Rentons and allowed them to pass on. 'My dear child, you cannot think how delighted I am to meet you. I wanted Rex to bring you here long ago, but'—lowering her voice— 'he seemed afraid of bringing vials of wrath down on your head! Never mind. I shall have my own way now and mean to see a great deal of you. And I am sure you will not refuse, will you, for your mother's sake?' Lady Roxley glanced down at the girl with keen approval. 'How like her you are!' she cried with a little sigh. 'And how beautiful you have grown! You will be the belle of my ball tonight. Oh dear, there is someone else coming. Keep near me, Fay, for I am going to introduce ever so many men to you directly. I see longing eyes wandering in your direction already!'

Mr and Mrs Renton had walked on into the ballroom and had not noticed that Fay had been detained; but Maud had, and was now searching the place with anxious eyes for a sight of Rex's tall figure, and suddenly seeing him in a doorway, she beckoned eagerly to him to come to her. He obeyed at once, with much precipitation. Of course, he expected to find Fay behind the voluminous folds of Mrs Renton's ruby velvet gown.

'So, you have arrived?' he cried, greeting them. 'I was looking out for you. But where—surely Miss Calderon has come too?'

'No,' answered Maud. 'At least, that is to say—Come and dance, Rex,'—she said suddenly—'and I will tell you all about it, and what has kept Fay behind.'

Maud considered Lady Roxley's appropriation of Fay a most fortunate chance. And though wild throbs of jealousy rose up in her heart at the sound of the Countess's cordial greeting, still the fact helped her wonderfully in her endeavours to keep Rex and Miss Calderon apart tonight. She threw a furtive glance at the doorway; she was so afraid her cousin would catch sight of the small, graceful figure in her satin gown that she put her arm in his without waiting for a reply, and he was obliged to take her into the middle of the room and dance. But he only took a few turns, for, besides his anxiety to hear news of Fay, he felt a little exhausted; Maud was such a particularly heavy partner. As he stood out, somewhat tired, a vision of loveliness flashed by. Rex caught his breath. He knew and always thoroughly realised Fay's charms, but he had never before seen her look quite so beautiful. So she *had* come, after all, and— she had forgotten her promise and was dancing with someone else.

He turned sharply to Maud. 'Why, there is Fay—Miss Calderon, I mean. You said she was not here!'

'I never said so!' answered Maud sulkily, for her envy was growing with every minute. She knew Fay's partner by sight and recognised him as the young Duke of Melcourt, and to think—to think he should have been introduced to that wretched girl—only her sister's governess!

'I certainly understood you to say so,' said Rex gravely.

'Then you could not have been attending much!' snapped Maud, and then quickly changing her tone, 'Oh, Rex! Rex! Why are you so blind? Why do you allow yourself to be hoodwinked so easily? I tried to warn you once, but you would not listen. If you only knew that girl as well as I do!'

'What do you mean, Maud?' Rex threw his head back with a haughty gesture and a dark flash lit up his eyes. 'I will not listen to any insinuations. At least, accuse Miss Calderon openly if you do so at all.'

Maud faltered and turned away with well-feigned hesitation. 'It seems rather like betraying a confidence,' she began, 'but still, for your sake, Rex. It was only something Fay said to me this evening in the carriage coming along.' She paused a moment, but seeing Rex waiting expectantly, she went on. 'She asked me if I were engaged for any dances with you, and when I replied no, she answered, "Well, I wish I were not either." It is true,'—she said, breaking off suddenly—'that you had asked her to keep some?'

'I did,' answered Captain Renton shortly, and his face was as a mask; all expression had died out. 'Pray go on. That is not all you have to tell me, is it?'

'No-o! Naturally I asked her why she said such a thing. I thought it so kind and considerate of you, because, of course, she would feel out of it—'

'What reason did she give?' interrupted Rex impatiently.

'She said she was sure to meet many of her friends here, because Lady Roxley had known her mother so well. She is very proud of the connection. But of course, as it was through you that she procured her invitation, she felt duty bound to promise you the dances you asked for, in spite of the fact that there were certain to be many partners she would infinitely prefer to you. She begged me not to mention a word of what she said, and I should not have done so only—Rex, I hated to think you should be so deceived!'

Captain Renton leant back against the wall. Her news did not seem to have had much effect on him. He was gazing calmly on the festive scene and the ever revolving throng.

'She has evidently found one of her grand friends already,' went on Maud spitefully. 'She is trying to reduce the Duke of Melcourt to subjection with her many wiles!' For the two had passed, gaily chattering, and there was a huge admiration growing in the young duke's eyes.

'The dance is over,' said Rex restlessly. 'I will take you back to my aunt.'

'Oh, it is so hot here in the room. Let us go outside,' begged his cousin.

But Captain Renton did not answer. He took Maud to the further side of the room and, without a word, left her there, standing with a background of a ruby velvet gown. It might not be an altogether ineffectual background to a light-blue silk, but it is a combination one would speedily grow tired of. As Maud knew no one to take her away and give her a change of scene, she was forced to remain with her mother for the rest of the evening. Two or three strangers were introduced, but only one turned up for his dance, and speedily brought her back to her mother when it was over.

Maud's eyes grew tired roaming about among the crowd of guests, seeking vainly to light on a face she knew and always returning to be disappointed. Not that she was not able to put a name to at least half the company present, for she knew the county people well by sight. But alas! There was never any recognition in their glances when they turned her way. After all, it was better to go to a function where all the townspeople were invited; when the men of that class were only too proud to dance with Miss Renton of the Manor. She ought to feel honoured at being asked to one of the exclusive castle functions, she knew, but then, it was not much pleasure to sit by her mother the whole evening looking on. And to make matters worse, there was that horrid little Fay Calderon dancing every dance, more sought after than any girl in the room, and Maud would have given ten years of her life to have spoken to even one of her partners. The only satisfaction Miss Renton had was the feeling that, at any rate, her schemes had been successful. Rex seemed to have vanished from the ballroom, and he and Fay had not even met. Yes, she had separated those two, and perhaps Rex would turn to her in his disappointment, and she might catch his heart on the rebound.

Meanwhile, Fay was enjoying herself immensely. True, she had been very sorry when she heard that Rex could not spare her a dance, but the feeling of disappointment soon wore off in the pleasure of dancing again and in the atmosphere of undisguised admiration she aroused everywhere. She had been a scorned governess for so long that it was absolute happiness to take up her position again, and in the set to which she by right belonged. She wondered very much as to what had become of Rex and why she saw so little of him.

Towards the end of the evening, a flounce of lace got torn off in dancing, and Fay hurried away to have it sewn on. On her return, she passed through a long corridor and suddenly came upon Rex, standing alone by the open window with a grey look of desolation on his face.

'Captain Renton!' exclaimed Fay, surprised. 'What are you doing here? Why are you not dancing?'

He turned around, startled at her voice, and stood looking at her for a moment, spellbound. The moon was shining in through the window, lighting up her sweet face and gleaming satin gown. She looked like some dainty fairy—a very moonbeam materialised.

She wondered at his silence and went up and touched his arm.

'Are you ill?' she asked anxiously. But her touch electrified him, and he shook off her hand rather roughly.

'No, thank you,' forcing his eyes away from the upturned face. 'I hope,'—with chill politeness—'that you have been enjoying yourself?'

'Oh, so much!' she answered, wondering more than ever at his tone. 'Captain Renton,' she went on, 'you seem so strange. Why are you not dancing? I am sure something is the matter!'

His wayward eyes returned to her face, lingered there, and stayed. Could those beautiful dark eyes indeed harbour deception?

'A promise is a promise,' he said, still coldly. 'I do not care to be cast aside like an old glove!'

A bewildered look broke out on Fay's countenance. 'What do you mean?' she cried. 'I quite understood your message. It was only natural that you would not have a dance to spare for me!'

Renton frowned. 'Message?' he repeated. 'I sent no message.'

'Oh, but you did. You forget—the one in Maud's letter—don't you remember?'

'I never wrote a letter for Maud.'

'Never wrote to Maud?' Fay echoed. 'But she told me so herself!'

'She told you that I had sent a message?' he said slowly. 'That I should not, after all, be able to keep you a dance?'

Fay nodded.

'And you believed it—Pshaw! Who am I that I should talk? I, who have been gulled in the same way, and successfully too! Tell me,'—he took her hands and drew her towards him—'did you tell her you regretted having promised me any dances?'

'No, no!'—half-frightened at his vehemence—'What can you think of me to ask such a thing?'

'Curse her!' muttered Rex below his breath. 'Here she has ruined my whole evening and given me two hours of the keenest torture I have ever experienced. But how should I suspect—suspect that my own cousin could be guilty of such a despicable act?'

Fay was trying to release her hands, but he held them all the firmer.

'No,' he cried passionately, 'I am not going to let you escape me again. Fay, I love you!' And his eyes seemed to burn into hers. 'Heaven only knows how I love you! I scarcely realised how much myself until tonight when I thought I had lost you.'

His arms closed around her, and she did not resist, and his head bent lower and lower until their lips met.

'Once before I found temptation too strong for me, do you remember, Fay? Ah, how often I have longed to repeat my offence and only was deterred by the fear of frightening you away!'

He bent his head once more, and the cool air of the beautiful spring night blew in upon them, and Fay forgot her dances and her partners and lived only in the present moment, which seemed to be brimful of happiness. And there the two stayed until Maud searched them out and in cold tones told Fay it was time to depart.

11

THE DAYS WENT ON, but Henry Renton was still unsuccessful in his search. The Yews was now nothing more than a desolate ruin, and the grounds a wilderness, yet day by day he grew keener, and neglected his business more and more, until at last he gave up going to his office altogether. And so, money ceased coming in, and poor Mrs Renton fell into despair over her heavy debts.

One evening, Henry Renton had fallen asleep after dinner. He had suffered of late from insomnia, and the shooting pains that ran through his head began to frighten him.

But this evening he slept, and Old Pete's ghost came to him in a dream and pointed to a tree, under which the treasure was hidden. In this dream, he dug down deeply until his spade grated on an iron box, and he awoke with a wild cry of delight. He started up with the dominating idea to try and verify this dream. Not a moment must be lost. The vision had been sent to help him.

He hurried out of the house just as he was, without his hat and without the knowledge of any member of his family. He raced along the road and arrived at the tall iron gates in a breathless, panting condition.

In the warm spring night, the Yews bore a terribly dreary aspect.

The dilapidated walls, the atmosphere of desolation which surrounded it, the dark avenue of trees which bordered the drive, nearly all dead or dying, because their roots had been cut at and killed from the excavations.

Renton paused a moment and looked around him with a shudder. The effects of his dream passed from him for a moment, and the awful uselessness of the whole thing was borne in upon him.

What if, after all, he never found the money? He had wrecked his business and wrecked his health, perhaps, for a mere idea. The still silence of the starlit night seemed to calm him, and the result of his rashness appeared to him with startling force. He put his hand to his head with a low moan.

A slight sound struck his quick ear, and he turned at once in the direction from whence it came. It was over against the east wall, and the sound was a rustle—a faint rustle, scarcely audible except to an overstrained ear.

As Henry looked, suddenly an indistinct outline of a dark head appeared over the wall, then a body, which stood at the top. For a second, the figure was clearly silhouetted against the sky, and then they dropped noiselessly down on the ground below. Immediately all thoughts of a soberer kind fled from Henry Renton. A throb of fury shot through his feverish brain, and murderous intentions rose in his heart.

Who was this intruder who dared to invade the sacred precincts of the Yews? This person who clambered over the wall, scorning or avoiding the many pieces of broken bottles with all the ease of habit? Was it possible that, while he tried to rest at home after his weary labour of the day, another took possession of the place and sought his treasure?

He crept along the wall, hiding himself in the shadows, a fierce, cruel gleam in his eyes, but when he reached the point where the figure had stood, nothing was to be seen—no sign was there of human nature. He stood there alone, seeming the only living thing in that garden of desolation. But no, there was again a sound, and Renton could with difficulty repress a scream as he looked up and saw a flash of white in the distance, floating towards him, seeming to grow in height and magnitude and horror.

For a moment that terrible, paralysing feeling which had assailed him before took possession of him, but with a masterful effort he threw it from him. After all, he argued, what harm could the spectre do him? Perhaps it had come to fulfil his dream and show where that luckless money was hidden.

And so he kept still in the shadow of the wall and tried to still his chattering teeth.

Nearer and nearer came the white figure, but there was no longer any appearance of floating. Instead, it came onward with a very human stride, and the gravel crunched beneath its feet. As it passed by the figure crouching by the wall, a hand of flesh and blood was stretched out to pick up a spade which lay hidden beneath a tree.

A sudden light broke in on Renton's brain, and his awful, superstitious fears left him. He connected the dark figure climbing the wall and the simultaneous appearance of the ghost. His limbs still trembled beneath him, but it was with rage now instead of fear. With a wild cry of frenzy he sprang, and his fingers fastened around the figure's throat.

'You confounded villain!' he cried hoarsely. 'You treacherous fiend, to come here like a thief in the night, to rob me of my treasure!' With each exclamation his grasp on the ghost's throat tightened, and he shook him as he would a rat.

The ghost struggled in vain. There was not another living soul within a mile. The terrible loneliness of night lay over all. It would be no good crying out for help: who would hear? Or, if there were a chance passerby, they would attribute the scream to the spectre who haunted the Yews and only hurry away quicker.

The poor ghost seemed to be caught in his own toils. He was choking under the grip of Henry Renton's long, bony fingers, and yet, through the round slits in the white mask he wore, he could see the murderous gleam in the other's eye.

He emitted a groan.

'Father!' he cried in a muffled voice. 'Father, don't—don't kill me!'

Henry's grasp relaxed suddenly, and the words seemed to sober him.

'Who—who are you?' he cried hoarsely. He roughly tore the sheet from the face of the ghost and disclosed the countenance of his son Philip.

For a moment the elder man paused, as if paralysed.

'You?' he gasped, scarcely believing the evidence of his own eyes. 'You?'

'Yes,' answered Philip sulkily, his eyes drawn with pain. 'And why not? I offered to help you and you rejected me with scorn, so I determined to have a try on my own account.'

'You treacherous young devil!' cried his father, with blazing eyes. 'And so you have been here night after night, have you, to try to steal my property, you thief! To think that you are a son of mine, you–'

'The money was left to whoever found it,' broke in Philip, trying to bluster. He felt braver now that those fingers were not encircling his neck.

'Out of my sight,' roared his father, 'or I will kill you! Do you hear? Out of my sight, you contemptible scoundrel, and never come near my house or darken my doors again!'

Philip needed no second bidding. The sight of his frenzied father terrified him, and he fled before he could feel again the touch of those icy fingers on his throat, and with terror, he managed to scale the wall and disappear behind it. Henry Renton was left alone with his rage in the midst of that silent garden.

12

It was a stormy night, and the wind was raging. Fay sat by Rebecca Grey's bedside in the little cottage on the cliff, for Rebecca was dying.

The girl had been every day to see her during the last week and had nursed her tenderly, but today she seemed so weak and feeble that Fay did not like to leave her, and so she decided to stay the night. In the present state of chaos which the Renton household was in, she knew she would not be missed. So she merely sent a note around to Rex at the castle and asked him to come around in the morning.

'I have left you all my money, dear,' Rebecca had said to her once, 'and the cottage too, and everything in it. So you need no longer depend on the Rentons for a livelihood.' And Fay sighed now as she looked at the old woman and feared how soon she would leave her.

Fay sat by her side while she slept, while the wind raged and moaned outside. As the night came on the gale increased, vivid flashes of lightning lit up the sky, and the roar of the angry sea grew deafening.

In the hush of the sickroom, the storm seemed almost more fearful. Fay put her fingers in her ears and buried her face in the pillows. But she could not shut out the sound of the blast, which seemed to shake the cottage to its very foundations, and the lightning appearing violent in its intensity scarcely ceased for a moment.

A horrible trembling seized Fay. She was so terribly isolated from nearly every living thing. The fisherman's girl who generally stayed with her had gone to see her parents late in the afternoon and had never returned, evidently being kept at home because of the severity of the storm.

With difficulty, Fay repressed the inclination to shriek aloud in her fear. She rose from her chair—it was impossible to keep still—but as she did so, a still more furious blast swept around the house. It seemed to shake and sway backwards and forwards, and then a violent crash sounded above and below and woke up the echoes of the night.

The girl clasped her hands tightly together and turned her white face towards the bed. She could not understand what had happened, only she felt that the cottage would not hold up much longer against the violence of the gale, and soon both she and the old woman would be buried among the ruins.

Rebecca moved uneasily, and at once the current of Fay's thoughts was turned. She forgot herself—even forgot the terrible fear which had assailed her a few moments before—and was back in an instant by the bedside.

The old woman began mumbling incoherently, and Fay sighed, for the doctor had told her in the afternoon that nothing could be done. She had never been face-to-face with death before, and here, alone as she was, it seemed to her infinitely terrible.

Rebecca's voice grew weaker and weaker, and then she closed her eyes, and the girl thought all was over, when suddenly the old woman sat up in bed and regarded her with fixed eyes.

'The fifth brick from the fireplace, ten from the floor. Don't forget, Fay—five and ten. Don't forget.'

And then, with a long drawn-out sigh, she fell back on the pillows, and Fay, with a low cry, threw her arms around the lifeless body of her old friend.

YEARS SEEMED to have elapsed when consciousness again returned to Fay. The wind had ceased; outside the dawn had crept in smiling, and all the elements appeared to combine to ignore the terrible ravages of the previous night.

Had it all been a terrible dream? She raised her weary head from the bed and shivered, for her fingers had touched the cold, dead hand of Rebecca, and the full remembrance of that terrible night returned to her.

She went to the window and glanced away at the distance. The sea was going on lazily, lapping the sand with gentle little ripples. It seemed to have forgotten its furious anger of the night before. Outwardly all appeared calm, except for a few stones thrown up on the cliff by the gigantic waves.

Fay sighed and, with a tender, loving look at the bed where Rebecca lay, peacefully resting in her long last sleep, she opened the door and went out.

Recollections of the previous night came back to her, and she began to wonder what had happened to cause that terrible noise that sounded as if the whole house was coming down, and which had even disturbed the old woman from her deep sleep.

She opened the kitchen door and went in, and at first could not make out what had occurred. The place was covered with dust, large bricks were scattered here and there, and the walls on either side of the fireplace seemed to be tumbling down.

Fay walked cautiously about, still rather puzzled. But when she went outside the cottage, she understood. In the fury of the gale a chimney had been blown down, but with the wind fortunately coming from the opposite direction, it had fallen away from the cottage, instead of on it, otherwise the place would have been in ruins.

Fay went indoors again and looked about curiously. She pushed a brick away with her foot and saw something gleaming golden amidst the dust.

She bent down in surprise and picked it up. It was a sovereign— yes, actually a sovereign. But what could it be doing here? A few steps off she saw another, then another, and just under the wall to the left of the fireplace was a whole heap of the same gold coins.

Fay felt she was in a dream. Had it been raining gold during the night? Else how could all this money be strewn about the floor?

Fay glanced at the wall above them. One brick had fallen out, evidently shot forward through the shock of the falling chimney. The hollow was just beneath the level of her eyes, so she stooped down and peeped in.

To her surprise, she saw a small aperture had been cut out. The missing brick had apparently only formed the entrance. She put her hand in and gave a little cry of surprise, for it rested on another little heap of gold. What could be the meaning of it all?

She took hold of another brick and carefully dislodged it. It had evidently been done before, for it yielded easily to her touch and enabled her to explore further. Now she caught sight of a small square box, lying on its side, and drawing it out, she perceived that the stream of gold must have originated from it, for it was filled to the top with sovereigns, and must have fallen over when the brick was displaced and the lid became loosened.

It was a most ordinary tin box, and Fay looked at it in perplexity. She plunged her hand in and pulled out heap after heap of gold, wondering if there was anything underneath to explain how it had come to be there, and to whom it belonged.

But she took some time to get to the end, for under the gold were banknotes—banknotes for £500 each. Fay counted them. A hundred and sixty—£30,000! She gave a little gasp of astonishment, and her breath came more quickly.

One more piece of paper—only a small half-sheet—and Fay took it out and read it.

'To the finder of this box I bequeath all its contents. The reason I hid it in the chimney-corner at the cottage is that it may not fall into undeserving hands. I know that whoever discovers the money must be one who is good to my old housekeeper and visits frequently at the cottage, trying to gladden the evening of her life. If, on the other hand, Rebecca is isolated, and no one comes near her, she has my orders to leave the cottage and all its contents to the Axton Hospital.

    —Peter Renton.'

And then came the signatures of two witnesses.

Fay sat down in her chair; her slight figure trembled, and her head swam. She had found in ignorance, through no trouble of her own, what Henry Renton had ruined himself to find, what he had given up months of days to discover. What Philip had toiled for night after night in vain. She had found the £80,000—Old Pete's hidden treasure!

It was not much later when Rex appeared, and he paused astonished at the sight of the money and notes.

'Have you been robbing the bank?' he asked.

'No, no!' she cried excitedly. 'It is Old Pete's money—the hidden treasure—which I have found! Oh, listen, and I will tell you —at least, when you have said "Good morning".'

And when this had been done to her satisfaction—and his—she told him of the old woman's death, and the wonderful way she found the money.

'I don't want the money, Rex,' she said. 'It belongs properly to your family.'

'It belongs to no one but you,' he answered, when he had read the piece of paper written on by Old Pete. 'It is not in your power to give it away. Besides, who has a greater right to it than she who tended and nursed Rebecca through her last illness?'

And he stopped and kissed her small, pale face, with a passion which startled her, and then he sighed and walked over to the window. The finding of this money brought no pleasure to him—it somehow seemed to set a deep gulf between himself and Fay.

WHAT MAKES A BOY A GENTLEMAN? Not merely lifting his hat to the ladies he meets, although that may be one sign, provided he lifts his hat to his mother and sister also. The real sign of the true gentleman is gentle unselfishness. Does he seek the good of others first? Is he brave and tender in caring for those weaker than himself? Does he show respect and courtesy to his mother, and to those older than himself? Then put him down as a gentleman of the true school, whether his feet be shod in patent leather, or he have no shoes at all.

IT WAS THREE MONTHS LATER, and Fay had been staying with Lady Roxley in Scotland. She was sitting alone on the terrace. The men were out grouse slaughtering, and the rest of the party was scattered about the castle and its grounds.

Fay had brought a book out to read, but it lay neglected in her lap, and in the soft sunshine of the August afternoon, her thoughts had flown back to the events of the last half-year and the wonderful changes that had taken place.

She, who had been a despised governess, was now an heiress, going to marry the man she loved, and the wedding was to take place at the Countess of Roxley's house in Grosvenor Square.

She thought of the people she had lived amongst and

shuddered, for disaster had overtaken their thirst for money in such a terrible way. The fearful rage which had overpowered Henry Renton when he heard the money had been found unhinged his mind. Something had snapped in his brain, and he was discovered a little later in the grounds of the Yews, digging mechanically and muttering childishly.

He was now in an asylum, and Fay had insisted on providing for Mrs Renton, allowing her so much that she could live in comfort for the rest of her days. Philip found some occupation out in Australia, and it was only Maud who was discontented. Maud, who, in spite of her wiles and schemes, had not parted Rex and Fay; who, in spite of all her endeavours to prevent such a state of things, seemed obliged to settle down into old-maidhood.

Fay was suddenly startled from her reverie by a little rustle of leaves below the terrace, and, looking down, she saw Captain Renton making his way in her direction.

A glad smile of welcome illumined her face as he approached.

'Why have you come back so early?' she asked.

He put down his gun and rested his arms against the balustrade. A worried look was on his face and an expression of gloom in his eyes.

'I have come back early,' he answered, 'because I wanted to speak to you, and I thought I might find you alone at this time.'

A vague fear took possession of Fay. He looked so serious; she was afraid something dangerous had happened.

'What is the matter?' she asked anxiously. 'Has there been an accident or—?'

'No, no,' he interrupted quickly. 'It is only that I want to speak to you about our marriage—yours and mine.'

'Yes.'

Rex turned away from her upturned gaze, and his eyes wandered restlessly over the purple moor beyond.

'You see,' he began, 'when we were engaged, you were poor— poorer even than I, but your circumstances have changed so—Oh,

Fay, don't you understand? It is not fair to keep you to your word. You, with your beauty and wealth, might marry anyone in the kingdom. You ought not to waste yourself on a man as obscure as I.' His words came quickly, tumbling on the heels of each other in his anxiety to get them out, but his tone was hoarse and sounded unnatural.

Fay's head was bent low; she was tracing patterns on her gown with a small, white finger.

'Do you mean you don't want to marry me?'

'Not want to marry you!' he cried hotly, and then stopped. The matter must be dealt with in a practical way; he must keep his own feelings back. 'You know,' he continued more calmly, 'that it is only because of the money I say this.'

'But the money is yours as much as mine—if not more so. If I were not going to marry you, I should feel I was taking away your right. As it is, you are the only son of the elder brother, so you and your father have more claim than anyone else.' Her head was still lowered, and he could not see her face.

'The money is absolutely yours. I wish that it never had been, for it has come between you and me. You used to be my very own. The curse of gold never came near our love. Now everyone will look on me as a fortune hunter! You know as well as I do that the Duke of Melcourt is head-over-ears in love with you, and you could marry him tomorrow if you wished.'

'Why should you persuade me to marry a boy?'

'Because like any other human girl, you would be proud of being a duchess!'

She rose from her chair now, and he saw a mist of tears dimmed her sweet eyes. She stood by him, and her beautiful white arms stole around his neck.

'Oh, Rex,' she cried, 'I should only be proud of such a thing if you were the duke. As it is, I would rather be Captain Renton's wife than anyone else in the whole world!'

And all Captain Renton's good resolutions faded away like mist before the sun. How could he reason properly when imprisoned in those white arms? Who cared what anyone in the universe thought of him with those sweet lips so intoxicatingly near his own? He protested no more, but merely bent his head and kissed her passionately.

'JENNY WREN'

NELLIE CRUTTENDEN

Dates of Birth and Death — Unknown | Published from 1877-1926.

A woman of mystery who attempted to conceal her identity under a pen name, Jenny Wren published works in newspapers all over Australia. Although there are two women known to have written behind this literary mask, we believe that the author of this story was a woman named Nellie Cruttenden. Her surviving stories were published between 1877 and 1926, with a gap of thirty-seven years between the publication of her last two known works—a period in which she may have spent producing this substantial novella.

Cruttenden's short stories—which include "Frankie's Folly" and "Love's Sacrifice"—share features with Wren's work, including coming-of-age storylines centred on marriage, love, and duty, with level-headed women at their hearts. Such stories also share the writing style, tone, and signature wit of "A Man and His Money".

Corella Press is thrilled to have unearthed Cruttenden's work and for the opportunity to restore her to her rightful place in the Australian literary consciousness.

M'KENZIE'S GHOST

PUBLISHED IN THE SYDNEY MAIL AND NEW
SOUTH WALES ADVERTISER ON 14 APRIL
1883.

SILVERLEAF

M'KENZIE'S GHOST

It was in the month of April, when the summer with its long days and intolerable heat had become a thing of the past, succeeded by sunshiny days with cool breezes and heavy night dews. A welcome change, for during the long summer on the plains of the interior, the nights are dewless. Dan Cassidy and I were camped out on the edge of a thick scrub, moonlighting cattle. Who and what I was is of very little consequence to anybody; the matter of the greatest moment to me was the fact that I was 'down on my luck.'

My colonial experience had resulted in a very short time in empty pockets, and my principal concern was to get them replenished, or to learn how to get on without the needful, which I had valued so lightly and got rid of so easily. I was now on a visit to my friend Delamere at his station some four-hundred miles from Sydney, on the great grassy plains where for miles and miles not a hill is to be seen. The only variation in the landscape is the difference between vast plains, box forests, and pine scrubs, and where the eye aches for the changes of hill and dale, and rolling river, and the many beauties of wild and rugged scenery. Delamere and I had been chums at school in the bygone past and fast friends afterwards, but we had been parted many years, during which he had gone up whilst I had been going down; I dissipated my patrimony like the prodigal son in riotous living, while my steady friend had, by dint of perseverance and hard work, added little by little to the very slender means with which he began life. By the time of which I write, he was a prosperous man, with a good run, well secured, improved, and happy in the possession of a charming wife and three lovely children.

With as good or better abilities than my friend, with greater means and more chances, I had let all life's prizes drift by me. I had forfeited the love of a noble woman, who had given me up because, as she said, she dared not risk her life's happiness with one she could not respect. So here I was, at the age of thirty-five, without means or prospects, and availing myself of my friend's invitation whilst awaiting remittances from home. I was anything but sanguine. From the tenor of my father's last letter, as he said in justice to the rest of the family, he could do no more for me. Being a good rider, having been a daring fox hunter in the old country, I was ready and willing to assist my friend in the station work. So this is how it was that the stockman, Dan, and I were waiting, with what patience we might, stringing in the scrub cattle on to the plains to feed; other parties were stationed as we were, whilst another herded a mob of quiet cattle on the plains, in the hope they might act as decoys to entice the wilder animals to join them.

The run had been recently fenced and many of the scrub cattle had been left outside, a portion of the fence had been intentionally left open, and it was our objective to get these gentry in.

After supper we separated to await the rising of the moon and the advent of our unsuspecting game.

I attached myself to Dan Cassidy, stockman, horsebreaker, roughrider, and factotum in general as to horses and cattle. I thought he looked dubiously at me, as being a new chum, but he said nothing, and he knew that as far as going went, I could both stick on and go as if the Father of Evil was behind me.

'It isn't the goin'; any fool can do that,' remarked Dan

sententiously, 'it's the generalship as does it, to get scrubbers a man must be a good general; all you've got to do is to follow me; when I go aisy, aisy it is, and when I gives the mare the spur, go like the mischief. But don't go on your own account at them bastes like a bull at a gate, because if ye do ye'll lose every hoof of them.'

The waiting seemed very long to me; the moon appeared to be behind time, as if it would fail to keep its appointment. I fidgeted and fumed and looked at my watch repeatedly by the light of the fire.

'My watch must have stopped,' said I, 'it is not eight yet, and the moon does not rise till nine. Don't you think we would do better if we were to ride into the scrub and rouse them out? It is such slow work waiting.'

'Fair and aisy,' said Dan. 'Hurry never caught anything yet, barrin' flays, and I don't know but thems aisier to goin' steady at it; ye'll have worry and plenty before ye are two hours older, so just keep yerself in reserve.'

While he spoke, Dan kept puffing away at his short clay pipe, and, by the light of the fire, carved his stockwhip handle; this was an unfailing source of amusement and employment to him, and much time and labour had been expended upon it. The substance was the sweet-scented myall wood, and on it he had carved, in his idle moments, specimens of the fauna and flora by which he was surrounded—emu, swans, brolgas, snakes, trees, and flowers—all faithfully depicted in minute and beautiful characters, not in high relief, but so clearly and correctly as to show ability of no mean order. Use had put a fine polish on the whole. When I first beheld this primitive work of art I considered it perfect, but Dan always had something to do to it, and now was busying himself in elaborating the feathers of the emu, though he must have had keen eyesight to work in the uncertain light of the fire. I threw myself down, resolved to wait as patiently as I could. Yet thoughts— haunting, clinging thoughts, that would not be shaken off and would intrude, tormenting me with might-have-beens—made it terribly wearisome. Long ago I had found out that active employment is the great panacea for trouble and care—labour of some exhaustive kind which gives no time for fretting and fuming, and if it does not cure life's ills at least makes us forget them. But to wait here in the dim light, restless but inactive, with nothing to do but think, was maddening to one of my irritable temperament, more especially as conscience, that stern monitor, told me with still but never ceasing tongue that my troubles had been of my own making. I had, with a liberal hand, scattered the thorns on my couch and had no right to start and writhe at the sharp stabs they gave me.

'Tell me a yarn, Dan,' said I, no longer able to bear the silence and monotony. 'Something to pass the time and enable a fellow to shake off the blues.'

'Sure, Mr Stanley,' said he, 'ye've heard most of my yarns more than once, and I don't suppose you'd care to hear them again.'

'Oh, I don't care, tell me what you like. Your stories, Dan, are worth hearing twice, and that's more than I can say for those of most folks.'

'Did I ever tell you about that ghost I saw when I lived the other side of the Blue Mountains with Mr O'Mulligan?'

'No, but that's a nice pleasant subject to cheer up a man with who is down in the dumps; but fire away, a fine lively ghost may scare away the phantoms which haunt me so persistently.'

Dan laid aside his pipe, threw a pine branch on the fire, resumed his carving, and commenced his yarn.

'I wasn't always a stockman, though I've been amongst horses and stock most all my life. When I first come out from ould Ireland, sorry as the day I left her, I took service with Mr O'Mulligan as coachman. I liked the place well enough, but the missis's nerves was tryin'. She was always afeared of stumpholes and being run into, and kept a'telling me to look out for danger when there was ne'er a thing nigh, that I was time and again close up having a real accident.

'Well, the master come back from Sydney one day, bringing a painter chap from the ould country as had brought letters to introduce him. And the master, being good-natured-like, invited him to pay him a visit, telling him the scenery was grand, and he would be charmed with it, though what there was to look at barrin' hills, trees, and rocks, with a glimpse of the sea beyant, passes me, for houses was mighty scarce. There wasn't a decent bit of road for miles, and the stones were that bad that the horses was forever casting their shoes and breaking their feet.

'Well, when I was driving the master and him from the train, I heard him a'telling that there weren't no work for his profession, and that he was mortal sorry he ever set foot in Australy. He'd painted two pictures and couldn't get nobody to buy them; one I heard say was "Melrose Abbey in a Fog," and the other "Sydney in a Brickfielder." I saw them after—for he persuaded the master to buy them—and if thems pictures I could do better myself, for ye couldn't see ne'er a'thing in either of 'em but fog and dust. A gentleman says one day to the master, "Ye've had ye're pictures damaged, and most obliterated," and the master had to explain, but the painter chap said as he knowed nothing of art.

'Well, when he'd been there a week or two, and I seen as he looked rather out at elbows, I thought to a'done him a good turn. There was an ould dray that ye could not tell what colour it might have been, so little paint was left on it, and there was some water casks and tanks as wanted painting powerful bad. So I says to him one day when I was driving him to a place as he wanted to make a picture of—though it was nothing but a great rock with a tree overhanging it, with a tiny spring trickling out of it—

'"I can put ye up to a job," says I. "I knows someone as wants some painting done, and would pay well for it, either by the day or for the lump."

'"Who is it?" says he, quite brisk.

'"Why, the master," says I. "Sure there's our ould dray, and all the tanks and casks, they haven't had the last taste of a brush this many a'day, and if ye done them well ye might git the house itself to do both inside and out."

'Now, would yon believe it, sir, the painter chap, instead of being grateful, he first couldn't spake for passion, and then he called me all sorts of names and abused ould Ireland in such an indecent fashion that if he hadn't been such a mere third-paper of a fellow, not weighing more than eight stone, I'd a lam'd him down to rights.

'When we got back he ups and tells the master as I'd insulted him, but when I'd explained, the master saw at once as I'd been wishful to do him a kindness. But, lor! how he laffed, and I heard him a'telling the missis. Whatever he told the painter chap I don't know, but he comes out to me whilst I was a'grooming my horses and makes me an apology, so handsome that we was as good friends as ever. Poor chap, he puts his hands into his pockets, feelin' for what I knowed as well as him wasn't there, and blushed as he said, "Well, Dan, if I was a rich man I'd give you something worth having, but when I sell some of my pictures, I won't forget you."

'After this, I took him out more than ever. Though he were as nervous as a cat, it most ways happened that the places he fancied was always the hardest to come by.

'He'd gone a long drive one day, and the sun was a'going down, and I kept a'calling to him to hurry, as it gets dark quick in them mountains.

'"All right, Dan," says he, "in a minute." But he kept on working away at a great tree as had been struck by lightning, which showed he were a fool, for there was good timber close anigh him.

'At last the sun was gone, and it got dusk all at once.

'"It'll take us two good hours," says I, "gettin' back, for the road goes a long way round. We should a'made tracks an hour or more ago."

'"Is there not a shorter road?" said he.

'"Well, there is," says I, "but I'm afraid you'll find it mighty rough."

'"Oh, I don't mind that," says he.

'"And I ain't that sure of it, meself," says I.

'"I'm not afraid to trust myself to your guidance," says he, "and I'd like to go a new road. See! The moon is just rising, and I may see a new and beautiful view by her light. Let us go the short cut, I much prefer it."

'Well, truth to tell, I didn't care about this short cut, and I was sorry enough I'd spoke of it. Before my time, a man named M'Kenzie had hanged himself on an ould tree that had its branches right across the track. Poor chap! I suppose he tried a quick and aisy road out of this world and its troubles. However that may be, he didn't seem to find the next any aisier, for more than one told me that they'd seen his ghost a'hanging on that tree on moonlit nights.

'I weren't afeared of ghosts, never a one. More by token I seen too many in the ould country—ghosts with guns too skulking behind hedges, as it wouldn't be safe for an agent or landlord to meet—but all the same I liked the other road, especially at nighttime, but I didn't like to own up to that painter chap, so I started.

'Then I began telling him all about M'Kenzie, and how he'd put an end to himself on this road, and how we had to pass right under the tree where he hanged himself, for there was a deep gully on one side and a high cliff on the other, so there was no possible turn off.

'He was powerful interested and kept asking me at every tree if that was it.

'"Just the next turn in the road," says I, "a tree with a laning limb; it's close handy."

'The moon was pretty bright by this time, and as we drove round a rock, there was the tree with its white bark gleaming in the moonlight, and a gaunt limb barring the way, and, as I live, there was M'Kenzie a'hanging on it!

'The painter chap clung to me, his teeth chattering, and his face as white as ashes. He tried to spake, but uttered never a word.

'I plucked up spirits, though truth to tell my heart was in my boots. If it had been possible I'd turned round and drive back, but the road was too narrow, so I whipped up the horse, but he seen the ghost too, and Devil afoot would he stir, but my temper got up and I give him the lash. He made a violent plunge then a rear and a swerve, and the next I knew, the buggy, horse, painter, and me was all a'struggling and kicking together within a foot of the precipice. The horse soon kicked himself free and flew like a deer away from the tree. I looked back over my shoulder, and there was a ghost a'wavin' in the wind, and it seems to me as if it was coming down after us. So I just caught hold of the painter chap, and shouted in his ear, "Run, my bye, run, the Devil's after us." He needed no second bidding you may believe; he just did run, and I with him, and where'd we'd a'stopped it is hard to say if we'd not seen a light twinkling up on the side of the hill. We made for it, and was not long bursting in and barring the door, the people thinking as we'd gone mad.

'The painter chap just stepped over the flute when he stumbled and fell, fainting away like a child.

'The good woman, instead of bothering us with questions, first brought the painter to, then gave us some supper. She put before us some first-rate soup, and when I'd disposed of about a quart of it, I began to tell them of the ghost, and—would you believe it—this heathens laffed.

'"If ye don't believe me," says I, mighty fierce, "ye may go and see for yerselves. I'll take my oath that there's an ould man a'hanging on M'Kenzie's tree this blessed night."

'"True for ye," says one strip of a gossoon. "I'll go bail for ye; there's an ould man hanging there."

'"Then what the mischief did ye laff at me for whin I would ye?"

'"I laffed," says he, "because ye said ye'd seen a ghost. Now, I don't believe in ghosts, but I know there's an ould man there, for me and Tim hung him there this very forenoon."

'"Ye murderin' hounds!" says I, catching hold of the painter, "let's out of this whilst we've any life left."

'At this they laffed more than ever, till they shrieked again, one of them barring the doors so as we couldn't get out. I determined to sell my life dear, so, seizing a knife and putting my back against the wall, I says: "Come on, ye bloodthirsty villains! Dan Cassidy will make some of ye bite the dust," whilst the painter chap took up his empty plate and held it fore him like a shield, a'shaking all the time as if he'd the ague.

'"Don't make a fool of yerself, Dan Cassidy, man," says the ould woman, "the boys are just a'foolin' with ye. It's an ould man kangaroo as the dog caught, and nought else."

'"Twas no kangaroo," says I. "Wouldn't a kangaroo have a tail? This ghost had just two legs a'hanging down, and his two arms a'waving in the wind; if it were a kangaroo where was his tail?"

'"Why," says she, "in this here pot, and very good soup it made, as you ought to know."

'Then I saw how I'd been took in, and I remembered as how the ghost had powerful long legs, and only dawny bits of arms. I now laffed as loud as any of them and begged pardon, and we shook hands all round.

'The painter chap was so done up that he asked the old woman to give him a bed. Lads came along with me to look for the horse; we soon found him, for he had got the reins tangled in a bush. We then went to M'Kenzie's tree, and there, sure enough, was the biggest kangaroo I ever seen in them parts. I seen bigger here. I helped them carry it home. The buggy was so smashed up that I had to leave it till I could come with a dray, and I rode home bareback.

'I often heard tales after of the ghost being seen on that tree, and I've thought as it might sometimes be something not quite so innocent as the one we saw, for many a fat bullock and sheep disappeared, as I think them chaps could have accounted for, and that they hung the carcase on the M'Kenzie tree to scare folks off.'

Our fire had died down during Dan's yarn, and the moon had risen. Mounted on our horses, we sat like statues ready to intercept the cattle and prevent their retreating into the sheltering scrub.

We had not long to wait. The tramp of hoofs was heard, twigs and branches breaking, ceasing at intervals as if the cunning animals stopped to reconnoitre, and repeating as they became reassured; soon the whole plain was dotted with cattle of all ages, colours, and sizes. We had a glorious chase after them and succeeded in yarding a great number, some of which had not been in a yard since they were branded, and judging from their horns and hides, they might rank with the oldest inhabitant. They proved to be ugly customers at close quarters and quite as powerful to scare a new chum as M'Kenzie's ghost.

On reaching the homestead I found that the mail had arrived, bringing me a budget from England: a letter of stern admonition and rebuke from my father; loving entreaties from my mother and sisters; and the news that my old, parsimonious Aunt Betsy had 'shuffled off this mortal coil,' not making me her heir, as she would have done had I been more considerate of her whims and wishes, but leaving me sufficient to liquidate all my debts and make a modest start in life.

With a blessing breathed on the memory of Aunt Betsy, I started to build up my shattered fortunes. Delamere admitted me into partnership with a small share. I took up a 640 acre selection on an insecure part of the run, and on it I have built a comfortable dwelling, and with Dan as my right hand, I live in peace and contentment. News of my reformation and steadiness has gone home, and I am not without hopes that the broken links of my life will be mended and that a happiness, such as one short year ago I dared not even dream of, may be yet mine.

'SILVERLEAF'

JESSIE GEORGINA LLOYD (NÉE BELL)

Born 1843, Launceston, Australia – Died 1885, Coonamble, Australia.

Jessie Georgina Lloyd was born Jessy Georgianna Bell, one of a large family of brothers and sisters whom she was solely responsible for upon leaving school. During this time, Lloyd was also closely involved with the church, playing the organ and teaching Sunday school classes. At the age of 23, she married George Alfred Lloyd, a station manager and son of the merchant, businessman, and politician G. A. Lloyd. They had a daughter one year later and went on to have three sons. The family moved to a homestead near Coonamble, and at 35 Lloyd began writing short fiction, essays, and poems for periodicals. She used her income from writing to send her two eldest children to boarding school.

Lloyd completed all of her literary pursuits under the pseudonym Silverleaf, which evoked the same sense of outback wistfulness as the stories she wrote. She became a popular literary figure in Australian newspapers and in her community. A few examples of her work are the short stories "A Tight Fix" and "More Sinned Against Than Sinning".

At the age of 42, Lloyd died of a haemorrhage at her home after six weeks of illness. A large congregation attended her memorial service two weeks later, mourning the loss of a cheerful narrator of outback life.

Corella Press is delighted to recover Lloyd's authentic storytelling and share it with contemporary readers.

ACKNOWLEDGEMENTS

CORELLA PRESS™ acknowledges the Traditional Owners and their custodianship of the lands on which The University of Queensland operates. We pay our respects to their Ancestors and their descendants, who continue cultural and spiritual connections to Country. We recognise their valuable contributions to Australian and global society.

The University of Queensland thanks the School of Communication and Arts for funding this innovative opportunity for UQ's Writing, Editing and Publishing students to learn while working with an in-house teaching press.

We thank Catriona Mills of AustLit, Deborah Lee and Michaela Skelly of IngramSpark, Kathleen Jennings, Sally Wilson of UQP, Peter M. Ball and everyone at Avid Reader for investing their time, knowledge, and enthusiasm in Corella Press and its student interns.

The University of Queensland could not have published this book without the help and service of Artika Prasad, Acting Management Accountant for the UQ Faculty of Humanities and Social Sciences, and the guidance and resourcefulness of the dedicated staff in The University of Queensland Fryer Library, particularly Angela Hannan.

We thank our colleagues and teachers in the School of Communication and Arts and its Writing, Editing and Publishing (WEP) program for their engagement, advice, and support. Great appreciation goes out to the professional staff of UQ's School of Communication and Arts, in particular Alex Moran, Sven Fea, Dolores Element, and Alison Buckley. Nothing gets done without you.

GLOSSARY

Beat About the Bush

To approach a matter in a roundabout way; avoid coming to the point.

Beyant

Irish English. Variant of beyond.

Brickfielder

A hot, dry wind local to Sydney.

Canst

Archaic or Poetic second person singular of can.

Chantilly

A fine silk or linen bobbin lace.

Clodhopper

A clumsy boor; rustic; bumpkin.

Cloud
A light loose-knitted woollen scarf worn by ladies.

Coiner
One who coins money; a maker of counterfeit coin.

Coquette
A woman who tries to gain the admiration and affections of men for mere self-gratification; a flirt.

Dawny
Irish English. Sickly.

Factotum
Someone employed to do various types of work.

Florin
A silver coin valued at two shillings.

Flute
In architecture, a channel or funnel with a rounded section.

Fly
A light, single-horsed public carriage for passengers.

Gauntlet-glove
A glove with a cuff-like extension for the wrist.

Gossoon
Boy or lad in Irish English, from French *garçon*.

Gull
To deceive; trick; cheat.

Lam
To beat.

Messrs
Used as a plural equivalent of English Mr.

Mollycoddle
A person, usually male, who is mollycoddled; a pampered or effeminate man or boy; a milksop.

Myall
Acacia pendula, a type of wattle tree native to Australia.

Scout
To reject with scorn; flout.

Serge
A twilled worsted or woollen fabric used especially for clothing; cotton, rayon, or silk in a twill weave.

Somnambulist
One who possesses the habit of walking about, and often of performing various other acts, while asleep; sleepwalking.

Sovereign
A former British gold coin.

Tete-a-tete
A private conversation or interview, usually between two people.

Tuft-hunter
One who meanly or obsequiously courts the acquaintance of persons of rank and title.

Wend

To direct or pursue (one's way, etc.).

CORELLA PRESS

Corella Press™ is a teaching initiative of The University of Queensland's Writing, Editing and Publishing program within the School of Communication and Arts. Bringing new life to nineteenth- and twentieth-century Australian Gothic, crime, and mystery stories, student interns at Corella Press source fiction from early Australian periodicals to produce beautiful, collectable, and thrilling books for contemporary readers.

As its avian namesake suggests, Corella Press is playful, disruptive, dynamic, energetic, and unapologetically Australian.

'What we are doing is recovering stories that have not been published for 150 years and introducing them to a new audience. While so much Australian literature has been preserved, hundreds of stories will never see the light of day again. We are working hard to uncover diverse voices from the past, and in essence give a different perspective of Australian literary history.'

— DR KIM WILKINS, FOUNDER, CORELLA PRESS, THE
UNIVERSITY OF QUEENSLAND

THE CORELLA TEAM

Founder: Professor Kim Wilkins

Managing Publisher: Meg Vann

Acting Director: Dr Richard Newsome

Editors: Jake Allwood, Rita Braby, Lorraine Han, Patrick Keane, Krista Mullally, Sebastian Petroni, Lucy Turner

Designer: Peter M. Ball

Technical Producer: Daniel Seed

CONNECT WITH CORELLA

facebook.com/corellapress

twitter.com/corellapress

instagram.com/corellapress

COLLECT THE CORELLA PRESS
CRIME AND MYSTERY SERIES

BRIDGET'S LOCKET
AND OTHER MYSTERIES

BY WAIF WANDER

Mary Helena
FORTUNE

THE MILLWOOD
MYSTERY

Jeannie
LOCKETT

FROM SHADOW LAND
AND OTHER GHOST STORIES

Edited by
CORELLA PRESS

MAN OR DEVIL:
TALES OF THE AUSTRALIAN GOTHIC

Edited by
CORELLA PRESS

STORIES TO READ BY CANDLELIGHT
www.austlit.edu.au/corellapress

CPSIA information can be obtained
at www.ICGtesting.com
Printed in the USA
LVHW111628111021
700155LV00001B/79